LOVING SANDER

a carissima Bambolina

JOSEPH GERACI

LOVING SANDER

<u>THE GAY MEN'S PRESS</u>

First published 1997 by GMP Publishers Ltd,
P O Box 247, Swaffham, Norfolk PE37 8PA, England

World Copyright © 1997 Joseph Geraci

A CIP catalogue record for this book is available
from the British Library

ISBN 0 85449 231 3

Front cover: F. F. Walter, *Aubrey* (1954)

Distributed in Europe by Central Books,
99 Wallis Rd, London E9 5LN

Distributed in North America by InBook/LPC Group,
1436 West Randolph Street, Chicago, IL 60607

Distributed in Australia by Bulldog Books,
P O Box 300, Beaconsfield, NSW 2014

Printed and bound in the EU by The Cromwell Press,
Melksham, Wilts, England

Part One: Dilemmas

1. Monday Morning, February 26th

This morning when I awoke the first thing that passed through my mind was "My God, it's Sander's birthday Saturday and I haven't bought his gift yet." I lay in bed feeling heavy-headed, allergic, dizzy, sickly, probably from the sixth straight week of wind, rain, and completely sunless days. I could hardly face opening the drapes. Wind was whistling through the cracks of the patio door and the bedroom was cold. Amsterdam: seven a.m., still pitch black.

When I did struggle over to the living-room window and pulled aside the drape the street lamp, suspended by thin wires over the center of the street, swayed wildly back and forth dashing swatches of eery, yellow light against the sides of the buildings opposite. I was still in a bit of a daze and I thought, what if it were to break away from its mooring and crash through this window. Soefi brushed against my leg wanting his breakfast. I shook my head trying to rid myself of some odd foreboding and started into the bathroom but he tried to get under my feet and trip me. My routine had changed. I had not gone straight to the cupboard to get him his food, even before my coffee. He ran ahead of me and flopped on his side in my path. I picked him up reassuringly. Maybe I should go back to bed, then get up and try again.

I looked in my calendar. Sander's party was Saturday at four. His party — Sander turned twelve. I should shop this afternoon and get the gift out of the way. I knew precisely what I wanted to buy him. Twelve! Nearly two years of friendship already. Parties made him manic, narcissistic, obtuse. I should be looking forward to it, even slightly keyed up, as he would be all week: flushed, wild, but affectionate. Marijke would be fraught with maternalism and find the confusion a good excuse to be nasty to me.

Nastiness, hostility — they were just beneath the surface anyway and sometimes I let her get away too easily with remarks. It was my own fault. I didn't like confrontations and the Dutch loved their conversation, their talking about a situation. Around and around it went, on and on, like the rotating plate in an electric meter, counting off ceaselessly how many words you were using, never stopping. Marijke talking about it. Talking about Sander and me, Sander and her, and herself, and herself. And then at times the hostility. The permission. A price extracted for my friendship with him, extracted perhaps for control.

Soefi sat purring on the counter watching me open a can of his food. A wave of slightly nauseating fish smell wafted by my face. The tea kettle began softly its crescendo.

Sander at twelve. At the party his cheeks would be flushed; his fine, light brown hair tousled, a wilful frown pulling tauter the skin over his smooth, defined chin. He would want his gift. He might hug me quickly, a little embarrassed with the others around. At parties sometimes he smelled of perfumed soap. He would wear one of the expensive white linen shirts his grandmother had given him, open two or three buttons at the collar depending on his mood, no undershirt beneath, sleeves rolled up on arms brushed by white gold down.

There would be a lot of people at the party, Marijke had said. Why on earth did she want a large party? It wasn't altogether like her, especially the last year. She had started therapy after the divorce from Niek and had seemed to withdraw. If it had been Sander's idea I might have understood. She often gave in to him. But it had been her idea. Quite spontaneously too. Or so it seemed. The three of us had been sitting around playing the Dutch game Rummikub, and she had said, "Sander your birthday's coming. Let's have a big old-fashioned birthday party this year. Invite all your friends, the whole family too…"

"Yeh!" Sander threw the dice and rattled off non-stop a litany of names, but I don't think either of us thought she would actually invite them. To tell the truth, I was at first excited by the idea. I said, "God, yes; a big old-fashioned thing with a huge cake..." I didn't get any further than that. Marijke said, "You can come, can't you?" That was that. Could I refuse? The control again. Sander missed it all, babbling on and on about what we should have to eat, who should come, what games we would play, maybe make up some skits. I diplomatically kept my mouth shut and threw the dice onto the board. My policy was not to burden him with innuendoes, though sometimes it was inevitable. Sometimes I didn't want her to know I got them either. Let it be. Just let it alone.

I put the bowl of cat food down on the floor and stood over Soefi looking down. God! Maybe even Niek would be there Saturday. We hadn't discussed that. Marijke might play some game about his living with his mistress, and Sander would be edgy around his father. Yes, but that was only part of the anxiety. Should I go back to bed now that Soefi was fed?

I brought my cup of coffee with me into the study. I had been letting the mail pile up in the metal tray on the edge of my desk for several days, and as soon as I started going through it I knew why. At the top of the pile was a letter from my University with the proposed teaching schedule for the fall semester. I had not yet returned the papers I had to sign about my teaching load. A letter from my mother asking for the date of my return to San Francisco had gone unanswered for three weeks now. My American bank statements had not even been opened. I shuffled through the pile, letters from friends in the States, subscription notices for photography journals, university bulletins, a letter from a student of mine for whom I was acting advisor. I did not want to deal with any of it and threw it all back in the tray again. I paced the floor anxiously. Going back? Staying? Was my time here coming to an end? The conflict was breaking through the surface again, becoming more than an academic exercise of weighing pros and cons on two sides of a scale. But not today, I thought; I did not want to deal with emotionally laden issues. Decisions. Decide today? Stay? Sander? Emotions, conflicts threatened to break through the surface of consciousness and I forced them under again by sheer exertion of will. I made myself busy.

7

2. Shopping on the Damrak

I spent the morning in the library of the Kunstacademie working on the footnotes for my book and didn't get around to shopping for Sander until late afternoon. After all, my book was why I had come here in the first place, and finishing it before the fellowship grant money and my leave of absence ran out was the first priority. As I worked on it, poring over the texts spread open on the table in front of me, I had to admit that it was beginning to wear thin and seem a bit trite. Sander's gift and party, the decision of staying or leaving, gnawed at the back of my mind and kept me from concentrating.

My photography curator friend in Washington, Jonathan Coburn, had put me up to my book. While doing doctoral research on the origins of photography he had stumbled on some important early work by the English photographer Sherrington. Working in rural Holland in 1842 he had apparently taken the first salt print landscape photographs on the continent. Given the Dutch visual landscape traditions Jonathan's theory was that this was no coincidence and that Sherrington's inspiration could be ascribed to Dutch seventeenth-century painting. There were only a handful of Sherrington's prints extant, twenty or so at Princeton, and about forty in Leiden. He had read an essay of mine on the use painters made of photographs, and suggested I study Sherrington and the reverse link between painting and photography. Jonathan had more than enough government influence to get me a research grant, and enough academic connections to get me a seminar to teach at Amsterdam University, so I took leave of absence and ended up in Amsterdam writing *The Origins of Landscape Photography in the Netherlands.*

That road had also led soon after my arrival to Sander. His mother and father (they were not separated yet) ran a small, non-profit photography gallery. He was a photographer, she a painter and watercolorist. They attended a lecture I gave at the University about nineteenth-century photography in the Netherlands. A museum curator acquaintance introduced us and they invited me around to their gallery. Niek I knew was a very fine photographer, influenced by Dritikol, and I wanted to see more of his work. He had some recent female nudes I had seen in a recent group show and which I thought were very intelligent and fresh. Marijke's grand- father had been a famous sculptor and resistance hero killed in the war, and an article had appeared a couple of months before about her moody, psychological paintings. I went later that week to meet them.

Their gallery was a lovely space in the basement of an eighteenth-century canal house: parquet, polished floor, long white walls, a low, beamed ceiling, glass doors in the back wall opening onto a garden which in early November was still bright and green. I felt immediately at home as soon as I walked in off the street. We gathered around the desk to drink coffee and talk. They did not consider themselves business people, and — this was clear right away — they wanted to latch on to me for help and financial advice. As an American I suppose they thought I must know everything there was to know about making money through photography, not realizing I was nearly as impractical and idealistic as they. Before I knew it I was saying that I would curate a Camera Works exhibition for them. I must have been feeling good about being there, and gotten a bit carried away with the friendliness.

Niek was showing me some of his latest work, outdoor nude studies shot in mists and fogs, very romantic and delicate and a far cry from the geometric abstractions of his early work. He was not typically Dutch, a short, thin person with wispy strands for hair, a high forehead, somewhat sunken cheeks and overly intense eyes. He seemed to suggest somewhere some Russian blood. As we hovered shoulder to shoulder over the oak table, I smelled alcohol. He was already starting to drink too much.

Then Sander walked in off the street where he had been playing. Sander at ten. He stood on the other side of his father and peeked at me from behind Niek's protection. Sharp green eyes and fine, sandy brown hair silken and with a slight curl, all mixed up with strands of gold, sand crystals and sun; that prominent, willful, sharp chin; broad, high forehead, lined when he pursed his lips making him seem oddly aged. He looked very intelligent and quick-witted, a bit too edgy, like a nervous deer. I felt immediately I had to be careful with his sensitivity; perhaps it would keep me at a distance. His features were oddly askew, with that awkwardness of childhood when things do not all grow in the body at the same rate. He had a certain puckish smile and charm, but also something hauntingly moody and intense, perhaps drops of his father's exotic blood? A few beads of sweat above his lip. Very clear skin flushed from running. Thin body, bony shoulders, very narrow waist, though a bit hard to tell under the baggy sweater and old-fashioned, Dutch styled, loose farmer's pants. A rumpled kid, not a street kid — too refined to be a country boy, but a little too animal wild for the city. Perhaps he was a sea bird, delicate and graceful seeming but robust from heading against winds. Later I remembered a wild bobcat I had seen once on a hillside, running head down, fierce.

They owned a farmhouse in Friesland where they stayed on weekends. Big feet, the laces of his running shoes undone, as boys wore them. He played absentmindedly with the long fingers of his father's left hand, pulling at them, twisting them, squeezing them; it aroused me. When I glanced in his direction he was always looking at me, and even smiled coyly before looking away. He went out again to play without saying even one word to me. Nor did he come back into the gallery before I had to leave.

Sander at ten. The whole morning at the library he kept coming back into my mind and I had to look up references several times before I had them right. I would read a word and an association would flutter by; turn a page and see a photograph and remember something small he had done. Little gestures, a word here and there would intrude on me as if someone nearby had a radio that they kept turning up loud, and then down again, or as if some little child kept peering in my window. Distractions, though, tinged with anxiety.

Perhaps it was something about the party that was setting me off: Niek being there when there were so many decisions that had to be made about the gallery, perhaps their neighbors and my awkwardness about explaining who I was and why I had the right as Sander's 'friend' to be there, or perhaps Sander running about the house, being a bit aggressive and independent with me, the way he could be when his friends were there, a bit of a pain, but sexy. He could be so unpredictable, perhaps due to his current confusion over his parents' separation, or perhaps because of his encroaching puberty. At one moment he was moody, reserved, the other he begged that his aloofness be broken down, coyly sidling against me for affection. The best thing I thought was to go buy his gift, what every twelve-year-old needed — a Walkman, perhaps with a couple of rap tapes. My God, I thought, loving Sander at twelve was like trying to hold some thrashing cat.

At about two I decided to give it up for the day. Toon's trial was this week and as I was going to be an expert witness I thought I had better phone him and see if he was free to go over some details again. He was at home and could meet me later in the afternoon at a cafe near the stores on the Damrak where I was going to shop for Sander's gift.

The Damrak was crowded with tourists. What they were doing here in February in the rain I didn't know. It was too windy to open my umbrella and when I got off the tram I had to run across the street for cover, the cars not giving an inch, not caring about my getting drenched, dodging in and around them hardly able to see. Thank God for the hood on my jacket. I had learned about clothing here right away. Why should there be so many people on the street, on a weekday afternoon in a fierce rain?

Should I or shouldn't I buy him a Walkman? Maybe that was asking for his withdrawal, walking around with those things on his ears avoiding conversation, in his own electric world. So why was I doing it anyway? I could have bought him something else, a score of new shells for his collection; he might have liked that as much. Was I encouraging a little separation? Maybe I just wanted to please him. He'd lie in bed next to me reading and I would hear the music scratching its way through the headphones, dim, horrible, shrill little screeches that would irritate me a little as he avidly devoured his comic book. I would relax next to him, read too. Against the irritation I would summon up a little of my affection. Then it would be all right.

But why not be honest? I remembered the exact moment when I decided to buy him his Walkman — it occurred last summer, after the stay on Texel. A friend of his own age, Michiel, had bicycled over to his house to show him his new Walkman. We were out back in the garden. Sander wanted to listen. He was wearing new, bright blue Levis with nothing underneath, no shirt either, nor shoes or socks; he clipped the set onto the beltless pants; they were still a bit stiff and baggy and sank down with the weight uncovering the flat planes of his tanned stomach, navel, the pubic line of leg and thigh. He put the earphones over his tousled hair, dry from the sun, closed his eyes, flung his arms wide and began to do a very sexy dance. He would open and close his eyes to see if I was watching him. His arms were raised, bent at the elbow in something like a *czardas* pose, his hands closed in loose fists, and he churned his hips, twisting this way and that, becoming a little, visibly aroused. Michiel was embarrassed, his face reddening, unsure of himself and what to do. I went over to Sander and gently, hesitatingly, seeing if he would agree, lifted the earphones off his ears and put them on, the set still hanging from Sander's trousers. He put his hands over the earphones, pressing them gently against my ears, looking up into my face smiling. He leaned against me pressing gently. I had been trying to deflect Sander and ease Michiel's embarrassment, but there we stood, Sander tender and warm against me. I took off the headphones and handed them back. I said I liked the music, which I honestly did. Sander handed the set back to Michiel. A Walkman it had to be.

There were, within the same block on the Damrak, three electronic stores and I went into the largest. Not a very technical person, it hadn't occurred to me that Walkmans came in all sorts of sizes and prices. The salesman wasn't very helpful. He put a couple of different models down on the glass counter in front of me that were quite far apart in price, and when I asked him which was the better set he shrugged and looked away, though I think he muttered something or other about sound quality or playing time, or 'extras'. I chose a mid-priced one and insisted he take it out of its box and test it for me with batteries before I would buy it. He did this peevishly. Maybe it was the bad weather affecting everyone, maybe it was just Dutch service, always a little resentful, doing you the favor of waiting on you, not meaning to please. As he was ringing it up he said sarcastically (or was I imagining it): "A gift for your son? (Why did he say 'son'?) Do you want wrapping paper?"

"Gift," I answered simply.

3. Meeting Toon

As I left the shop I ran into Toon. He had just stepped off a tram, limping more than usual, and was crossing the street on the way to the bank before meeting me. He wasn't wearing a hat or carrying an umbrella and had pulled his head down as far as he could into the collar of his coat to protect himself from the gusts of wind and the stinging, icy rain. I hailed him and he hurried over to where I was standing, under the shelter of the shop marquee. He shook out the collar of his coat, grimacing. Perhaps the weather aggravated his injury. He had been in a motorcycle accident several years before and had badly injured his back and right side. He went through periods when he was totally laid up in bed and his friends had to wait on him, bring him meals, read to him.

The cafe next to Nieuwe Kerk was nearly deserted and we found a table near a window and radiator. It was very quiet inside; a large ficus plant hid our table. The greenery, the smell of coffee and cooking food made me feel better. But apparently not Toon. He really did not look at all well today, worse than the last time I saw him. He had gained a lot of weight and had not had a haircut for several weeks, and his long hair made him look more derelict than bohemian. He was clean-shaven though; even smelled faintly of lemon-scented aftershave lotion which I found a little out of character. He was over six feet tall and settled his large bulk with some difficulty into the narrow chair. I asked him a couple of questions but he hardly gave me an answer. His shoulders were hunched; he was scowling; he had dark circles under his eyes.

We had met at the Amsterdam Paedophile Workgroup meeting the second or third time I had attended. There is no exact English equivalent for *werkgroep*. Our 'task force', or 'support group' do not quite get the drift. It is a peculiarly Dutch invention: a group of like-minded (one might say, like-desired) individuals sitting in a smoke-filled room, drinking a lot of coffee and talking endlessly around a subject, which in this case happened to be mostly boys. The paedophile workgroups began in the early seventies, and by the early nineties when I started to attend there were about sixteen of them spread over the various Dutch urban areas.

The paedophile groups were neither officially sanctioned, nor interfered with by the police — at least, to the best of anyone's knowledge, although at times rumors abounded. Not much seemed to happen there, certainly never any organized discussions or guest speakers. The room was small and a bit shabby. The large front window would not open, and the door was kept closed so that the room quickly filled with tobacco fumes. A small bar had been built along one wall, which served beer, soft drinks and snacks. There were little round tables with candles in bottles such as I remembered from Greenwich Village Italian restaurants when I lived in New York as a student. Some people played cards, most just talked. These were, in other words, human societies, social groupings giving mutual support. Relationships were discussed, advice given, legal problems analyzed. There was friendship, openness, and solidarity.

The first time I went, only a few days after my arrival, I had some trepidation. I was with Dr Erich Born, an expert on paedophilia, with whom I had been corresponding and whom I had gone to see for advice before moving here. He knew everyone and was involved with everything. He had written the first book about the positive effects on children of sexual relationships with adults: interviews with two thousand boys who had been in 'paedophile' relationships. Of medium height, he had a thin wiry build and moved with quick steps. He kept himself fit by an obsession with swimming. To do something, he said, he had to permit himself to be obsessed. Already in his early seventies, he looked no more than fifty, although dying his hair Spanish black helped. He had been raised aristocratically in Switzerland; his father was a surgeon whose theory was that every child should be raised speaking at least three languages. He knew six or seven, which, as an American, I found intimidating. We are hardly raised with one and I have often wondered why our society so undervalued even its own language, not to speak of having little interest in others. Perhaps it was decadence, perhaps a form of autocracy?

I liked Erich's sense of community. I quickly saw that it was he who knew everything that was going on so that if you wished to stay informed it was a good idea to be friendly with him. He also spent a good deal of energy helping others and keeping them involved in the meetings and activities of the workgroup that he himself had co-founded. I saw a good deal of him, especially soon after my arrival, and when the relationship with Sander began to develop it was to him that I turned for advice. We were quickly on a first-name basis.

He had published two books on child sexuality and in the fifties a tract on paedophilia under a pseudonym. He had also in 1959 been one of the four founders of the 'paedophile movement', though he often made jokes about whether such a thing existed. He was fond of saying, "There are as many kinds of paedophilia as there are paedophiles." Recently, the final volume of his major tract had been published, under his own name. He liked to wear fashionable, expensive Italian boots and sweaters. He had a religious side and in fact in his youth had been the editor of a left-wing Catholic scholarly journal. He had made a very comfortable living as a child therapist, and though he was recently retired he still saw some children in private practice.

There were about forty men at that first meeting, more than I thought I would find, and some of them had brought their young friends. We joined one table, three men and a twelve-year-old boy playing cards. It was there that Dr Born introduced me to Toon.

I had seen him sitting at the bar when we walked into the meeting room. He looked preoccupied and was not talking to anyone so I had left him alone. There was something that I liked about him right away. Perhaps it was the scruffy beard, something held over from the sixties, his unkempt look, the scowl that masked a raw sensitivity. He should have been living in another era when his somewhat anarchistic idealism might have been considered socially possible. He saw me staring at him and frowned.

There was a small photo exhibition hanging in the room and I made the rounds. One I particularly liked, a lifesize triptych of a twelve-year-old nude boy that I thought worked exceedingly well: sexy, respectful, playful, insightful, and technically accomplished as well. Each of the three panels showed one-third of the boy's body. Framed in thin black wood they were stacked on top of each other to make a lifesized representation. The test to me was whether or not they worked as individual photos and I decided that they did. It was a hard job to pull off successfully.

Dr Born came over to where I was standing admiring the boy and the photographs and said that Toon had made it and would I like to meet him. I said I would and he took me over and introduced me. There was an empty bar stool next to him and I sat down. Born told him I was 'an expert' on photography and then left us to carry on. Toon denigrated his work and seemed embarrassed by the fact that I really was a photography scholar and even taught the history of photography in the US, but he also seemed pleased that I liked his work. He had a portfolio of prints with him and went to fetch them to show me. He had some legal difficulties and was selling them to help raise money to cover his legal fees. I saw right away that his work was uneven but brave and talented. In fact, the erotic work was better than the sentimentalized portraits and the flat, boring architectural studies. I picked out one, of a Surinamese boy of about eight or nine. He was wearing only a long white shirt, clearly an adult's, open on his slim, graceful nude body. He was holding a stalk of Queen Anne's Lace and I liked the way he had intensified the whites making the shirt and weed glisten, and somehow managed it all without being sentimental. I said I would buy it, and he said that the boy's name was Ashok. I only realized much later, in getting to know him, that telling me the boy's name was an act of great trust for Toon. They were involved.

I took the photograph in hand and we went to sit at an empty table. Toon said that Ashok was an Indian boy from Surinam. I asked if there were more photos, that I would like to see them, and we made an appointment for the following week. After that we began to talk to each other and meet regularly.

"Any new photos?" I asked him now.

"No," he said sullenly. "I'm not taking photographs any more."

The Nieuwe Kerk cafe was not crowded but I had to stand up to get the waitress's attention and call her over to place an order. Photographs had added to the current difficulties that now dominated his life.

He had been arrested a few months before upon a complaint from a woman social worker stemming from his relationship with Ashok, who was now ten. I had met Ashok several times and liked him a great deal. He was quiet, very gentle, graceful, and I would even say a little elegant. We'd had dinner together a few times at a Dutch restaurant near my home, a cozy place where everyone sat together at big tables, one salt and pepper shaker for ten people, passed back and forth in a cheerful way. People assumed that the boy was Toon's — perhaps adopted — son. Ashok brought drawing paper with him and another boy his age came over to watch; he generously gave the other boy some paper and use of his colored pencils, and made room to squeeze him in on his own chair. Conversation went between tables. I had found it all very inviting, *gezellig* as the Dutch can be.

The relationship had been going on for a year and a half before any trouble erupted. What had happened was that Ashok's father had lost his job because of illness, and a social worker, a horrible woman named Lucy de Wit, had been assigned to the family. I had myself run into her once while visiting Toon. We were in a market near his house and he pointed her out. Before meeting her, from what Toon had said, I had formulated a picture of someone bossy and slightly hysterical, the type who likes to interfere with things she should best leave alone, and I was not inclined to change that view after our meeting. We could not avoid her and I hung back when we stopped to say hello. She looked at me disapprovingly although she did not know who I was. She had a thin, tight, mean mouth; she bit her lower lip. I hated the way she treated Toon — condescendingly, with even a bit of scorn mixed in. She should not have had the job she had as a 'child protection agent'.

She had been visiting Ashok's family for a check-up one day and had found Toon there. He was just leaving but she had asked the family who he was in a seemingly innocent and friendly way, and the next thing he knew she was phoning him and asking him to come into the office to see her. Ashok's mother had said innocently that Toon and Ashok were friends and she immediately had decided to nose around.

She disapproved of Toon from the first, of his being around the family, of his friendship with Ashok, of his lack of a real job, of his appearance. She questioned Ashok. He said sometimes slept over at Toon's on weekends, and that seemed enough for her to 'suggest' to Toon that perhaps his relationship was not appropriate for Ashok. Toon is very quick-tempered. He tried to argue and she made threats. She was enough of a petty bureaucrat not to want to have her power contradicted. Why we glibly give such power over people's lives to low-level functionaries who do not understand much about human heterogeneity, though they think they do, I shall never understand. Toon made the mistake of underestimating her power and overestimating his security. He told her she had no right to interfere with his friendship with Ashok. In a way he was sadly right: she did not have the right, but she had the ability. A remark from Ashok, that he slept nude with Toon, was enough for her. She went to the police and lodged a complaint.

When two policemen came to his house to question him he was overly cooperative. They had come on a routine visit, with no search warrant, but they asked him if they could 'look around'. Toon said they could. I do not know why he did this; it was a fatal mistake. Under Dutch law he did not have to let them into his house unless they showed a warrant. Dutch law does not even make it illegal to lie to the police. Framed on the walls of his upstairs hallway (he lived in a rundown maisonette) were nude photographs of Ashok. Some were Toon's best photographs. In one Ashok was standing in a pond with mist rising around him. A morning sun lit the mist and the figure from the side. It was mysterious and mythical. It had been taken the summer before at a camping ground in France where they had gone together for a vacation. I would not in any way have called the photo pornographic although the sun fell across Ashok's midriff highlighting the fact that he was erect. This photo had led to Toon's arrest. The police found other nude photos of Ashok. The parents did not know about them. They felt — or acted — betrayed, took the social worker's side, and Toon was prosecuted.

In some ways the prosecutors were very fair to him, which I do not think would have been the case in other countries. Usually when someone is arrested for sex with minors they remain in jail until their trial, which in Holland means a maximum of three months. The sentence would then usually include time served. Toon's arrest had been nearly three months before, but because his father was sick with cancer and he was tending him he had not been jailed. The Dutch legal tradition is not based on excessive punishment, vindictiveness or revenge. The media also tends to conduct itself reasonably. It is customary not to list the names of the accused in the newspapers, but only to give their initials. This is not a law, but something they have voluntarily agreed. The news stories about Toon's case had kept very much to the facts. 'A certain TK of Amsterdam was arrested on several counts of sexual acts with a minor...' It was only a couple of paragraphs on page seven. Toon had not even lost his job at a printer — in fact no one at his work knew of his difficulties. It was the strain that mattered most, but when I came to think of it I thought how much better his treatment was here than in the US, where he would be slandered, lose his job and suffer other kinds of terrible violence. The same in any society where the justice system is based on hatred and vengeance.

I said, trying to cheer him up a bit, "My God, if you were going through this in New York your life would be a complete nightmare. Your legal bill would be a hundred times higher, your name would be all over the newspapers, you would lose your job and your family would be interviewed on TV and would no doubt talk in terms of everything being a tragedy." He grunted in a surly way. I asked, "So, is there anything new we have to go over?"

"No. I mean they'll definitely put me in jail."

"Perhaps not, because of your father."

"They'll find some fucking social worker to take care of him."

I felt I was not asking the right questions today, so I tried, "How is Ashok?"

That too was a mistake. A stream of curses against Lucy came out. "Wait, slow down. What happened."

"The bitch. She found out he was still coming over to my house."

"But the police had forbidden you to see him, I thought."

"His family doesn't have anything; They depend on me. I mean I was the one who was bringing food and clothes to the kids. So his mother was allowing him to come and pick up things they needed."

That was surely taking a risk. "So how did Lucy find out he was still visiting you?"

"She saw Ashok walking towards the subway and she

actually followed him and made him tell her where he was going."

"You mean she forced it out of him. God!"

"Wait until you hear. She grabbed his arm and squeezed it and they were right out in public on the subway platform and Ashok was frightened. She's a fucking monster."

An image flashed through my mind, of a frightened look passing over Ashok's face. Then suddenly the face was Sander's. I shuddered.

I changed the subject and asked, "What time do I have to be at the court on Friday?"

"The trial starts at ten, so you should be at the courthouse just after nine in case there's anything last minute to go over."

I was going to testify, as an expert on photography, that Toon's photographs were of artistic value and though they might be termed erotic, they were not pornographic. I had written out some things I thought I would say at the trial and took out my notes to go over them with him, but he was in such a bad mood that there was not much of a discussion, and I wondered why we had even met.

Toon had to leave and I asked for the check. I paused under the awning over the entrance as he lumbered off into the rain again, pulling his head down into his coat. The conversation had left me feeling vulnerable and shaky. Everything suddenly seemed hanging by a thread, and the feeling I'd had when I awakened in the morning, dull and unarticulated, returned again.

A memory flashed through my head, of Sander and I lying together on my bed watching television. He began to get sleepy, his head nodding, resting on my shoulder. I had felt peaceful. Sentiment had welled up within me. I had felt at that moment that I might sacrifice anything for him, had felt crazy about him, felt in love. But sitting there talking to Toon I wondered if I was just being sentimental. Was there any room for even one ounce of sentimentality in our relationship, given the status of things in the world around? Not just Toon, his situation, and the law, but Marijke, Niek, the break-up in the family — Sander seemed at times so inaccessible and yet that evening lying together, as I put my arm around him and he had let himself be drawn against me, I felt we just might be able to make a place for our friendship if somehow we could build some trust together. And was that only an emotional house of cards? Erich Born laughed at me sometimes, making me feel American. He had said, "Sander calls you every day and comes over to your house as often as he can, and you still want him to profess some sort of love for you at every opportunity. You know as well as I that that's just not what a boy does. Especially not Sander!" He had laughed and added, "Maybe not even what a Dutch person does whatever their age." Now, sitting in the cafe I suddenly felt angry and had to calm myself down: mad at myself, at society, at the world in general, and also mad at Toon, mad at him for making me think that reality was so tenuous, mad at myself for allowing myself to be driven by any of a number of these things to question my friendship.

Now, as I sit here writing, thinking over the whole day, I still feel disturbed. Toon's case, no matter what he feels about it, would be an incomparably greater nightmare in the US or any of a host of other countries. How could I ever contemplate such a relationship as I have now with Sander back in San Francisco? It is not a question I want to ask. It leads to too many others. Should I live here permanently? How would I make a living? Leave the US behind? Land of the free, the goal of everyone in the world: our sacrilegious myth of the Promised Land.

Before I came here I remember Erich Born saying to me that if I came for many reasons, for the quality of life, for my research, for the adventure of being in Europe at such an interesting time, and did not come for boys, I would come to feel at home. I took that to heart. Likewise, if I am going to stay I have to continue to insist to myself that I have to stay for the same range of reasons.

I needed to see Sander before Saturday.

4. Tuesday Morning, February 27th

I was sleeping in this morning, meaning that it was 7:30, when Sander phoned and asked if he could come over. I sat up in bed feeling heavy-headed, shook my head a few times, my eyes red with allergy, my throat scratchy.

"What's happening? What's the problem?"

"Nothing. Can I come over today?"

I looked at my watch. It read 'Tues 27'. The day was surely correct; a school day.

"It's a school day. What's up?"

His voice rose an insistent notch. "Nothing. Nothing's up. There's no school today. Teachers' meeting or something."

I was out of bed now, nearly dropping the phone as I grappled with the sleeve of my bathrobe. The floor and apartment were cold; wind whistled through the crack in the patio door; Soefi stretched and yawned, front legs extended, his back gracefully concave, tail arched.

"Can we go see a movie? *RoboCop*'s playing and you promised..."

I could feel his energy through the phone. "Yes, but I have to get some work done. You know, make a living, that thing that adults do?" My foot somehow could not find its way into the slipper. I was in danger of falling, and Soefi flopped in front of me.

"You can work all morning. There's a show at two o'clock. That's six hours of work..." His voice went into cajole mode. I knew it well, stubborn, firm, manipulative, seductive.

"Commmme onnn," he added.

I tried responsibility, his school work, his mother and permission, my own work that never seemed to get finished, the shopping that had to be done, but they were all a matter of form. The truth was that hearing his voice first thing had made me feel better, feel the connection. I knew that I would go all soft. I shook myself again.

"You have to ask your mother first."

"I did already."

I could hear morning sounds in the background — the clinking of cups, the whining of the juicer, cupboard doors banging shut, the radio playing a pop song. I could almost smell toast and coffee.

Sander shouted, "Mum, can I go?"

Marijke walking towards the telephone: "You have to do your school work this morning first and I don't want to have any arguments about it, and you make sure you're not bothering Will. He's got things to do too you know and can't just go off to a movie like that..." Her voice growing steadily louder, then taking the phone from Sander, continuing the conversation without a break as if I had been there in the room, "He's such a pest some time, he doesn't realize people have their own lives and work to do and can't just drop things to suit him..." I heard a moan from Sander, in the background now — Sander wanting to see me.

"I've been doing footnotes for two weeks now and can probably finish up the last of them this morning. I can work all morning and if I know I have only a few hours sometimes I work better."

"He doesn't need to bother you all the time. He can go with Michiel and some of his school friends to the movie you know."

Was she giving me a choice? I did not want a choice before my cup of coffee. I said, "It's all right with me if it's all right with you.."

"He bothers you too much and he can go with his friends."

Then, Sander in the background, "Everybody's seen *RoboCop* except me."

I said nothing, hoping to keep things simple, waiting. "It's all right with me," I finally said.

"Well, if it's all right with you..." Her voice lingered in the air. It was typical of Marijke not to give her permission without ambivalence, without insisting on my insisting before she agreed.

She said, "I have to do a few things this afternoon that can't wait, and when he hangs around the house all bored he just gets me annoyed and makes the house a mess."

Sander grumbled in the background, "I do not make a mess." I imagined him padding around in those floppy, fur-lined, green frog slippers of his. His eyes would still be a bit swollen with sleep, his fine light brown hair dishevelled. He would not have buttoned his flannel pajamas properly and the tops would gape, a button open, a small swatch of light brown flesh glinting through. Naked beneath, the old worn cotton would cling close to the curves of his body as he bent over the counter without sitting, eating too hurriedly his fruit and cereal. She put him on. Sander's voice, free of pleading, and a plan for lunch: he would come by my house at one. He hesitated. I wanted to get off the line and get things started. So what else now? There was something else. Probably his bloody gift, but perhaps something else. Something to talk over when we met. Perhaps Michiel was teasing him again. Perhaps his father had said something, insulting him, pressuring him, the only son.

"Anything else then? You'll be here at one?"

He was still lingering, perhaps still not quite awake? I waited. He said, "See you at one."

Work and Sander did not always mix. Mid-morning I stopped for another cup of coffee and realized I was making too many bibliographical mistakes: punctuation marks out of place, dates wrong, Dutch words misspelled. I was rushing to get finished, to have as much free time with him as possible, but it was free time at the expense of the book and I knew I should have been spending the day working. By twelve I was edgy and discontent with what I had done and was relieved when the door bell rang early.

I buzzed him in and went to the door. It was an exceedingly gloomy day, hung with what the Dutch call *motregen* — 'moth-rain', a poetic name for annoying, filmy, suspended rain that penetrates every stitch of clothing. The sun would not break through. Soefi sneaked between my legs to sniff the cool air and I picked him up. My building was not characteristically Dutch. Each apartment had its own outside door, connected by a stone-tiled garden area. The downstairs door slammed; Sander taking the stairs two at a time, bounding across the noisy tile walk. His face and hair were wet; the rain hanging on the ends of strands in perfect beads. He took the cat from me and Soefi's blue, slightly crossed, Siamese eyes looked comically suspicious. He turned his head to sniff Sander's face, red with the cold. Sander closed his eyes and held his face still and then put the cat down carefully.

"Come on, let's go. You're taking me to get to a burger and a coke."

"Take your coat off. It's too early to go out yet. The movie doesn't start for two hours."

He was wearing another of those black, rap group tee-shirts, slightly too small Levis with no belt, the prerequisite running shoes, laces untied, a very thin blue nylon jacket, though he did not seem to be cold. He smelled ever so faintly of sweat and rain. I put my arm around his shoulder and gave him a squeeze, but too filled with the urge to do, he pulled away and walked ahead of me into the living room.

He said aggressively, "I bet you thought I was lying."

"About what?"

"Not having school."

I tried to make my voice sound aggrieved. "I did not think you were lying. I just wasn't quite awake, and it is a Tuesday. Anyway, do you lie to me?"

"No, creep."

I laughed. "To tell you the truth if I thought anything at all I thought maybe today was Wednesday and you only had half-day school."

He was walking ahead of me into the study and sat down on the swivel desk chair swinging himself vigorously side to side. He wanted to be pushed around the apartment, one of his games. The cat was smelling his foot and he stooped and picked him up. Soefi settled in his familiar arms. He stroked his back gently.

He seemed a bit angry about something. I knew it would be hard to draw him out; that was the way he was lately — not easily made aware of his feelings or ready to deal with them; they seemed rather to pop above the surface like a suddenly freed cork. To love Sander, or any boy, was sometimes to have to strike the pose of mind-reader, surprising them with our ability to see what they were they feeling, divine what they were thinking. I sometimes thought, loving Sander was having to cultivate my own ability to suggest and foster consciousness in subtle ways, and I was not that good at it. I could see he was angry, but was quite sure that he most likely did not see it himself. It might be because Michiel was teasing him again about how much time he spent combing his hair, or even because he was worried about a blemish that had appeared on his nearly flawless skin. Sander for the past few months had become almost neurotic about certain things, what I called his magic-think: if he did not wear a particular shirt on a particular day some girl in his class would not like him and his whole day would be ruined. If he parted his hair in such a way his day would go fine. If a pimple appeared it was a bad omen. Things he did shaped the world around him. That was not exactly superstitious. To do something in a certain way because you believe it affects events and attitudes is to imbue everything with potential life, an animistic trait common not just in children. Did it go with the energy of burgeoning sexuality? Michiel liked to tease him about his superstitious quirks. If Sander was worried about the side of the street they should walk on Michiel would drag him to the other side. Perhaps Sander secretly liked Michiel or I to draw him out of his mad magical mood. I asked him several times if this or that was bothering him but did not get it right and finally dropped the matter.

Later, as we walked from the department store back to the cinema, Sander was still not saying very much. The wind was picking up. Did I detect a thin spot in the cloud covering? Perhaps there was a chance of the rain blowing over. I pulled up the collar of his coat and asked him if he was warm enough. I wanted to pull him within my coat, warm him, protect him. "You're awfully quiet today," I said tenderly. He looked up at me seriously, allowed me to squeeze his hand. We were near the cinema, and I saw Michiel lingering in front looking at the posters, obviously waiting for us. Sander had not even mentioned he would be joining us and on first impulse I was a bit put out. I had wanted the time alone with him and said hurriedly, before Michiel could hear, "We'll have supper together after the film. We'll have to call your mother first, though."

I greeted Michiel. He was all muffled up in a brightly colored parka, and bright green, wool scarf. The Dutch intermarriages with Indonesians have created a special, refined, beautiful breed of people. Michiel had dusky skin, chiselled features, pale blue eyes. He smiled warmly as we came up but Sander seemed nervous and in fact crossed to my right side so that I was in the middle. Sander had obviously invited Michiel to join us but was now avoiding him.

It was still a bit too early to go in so we walked over to Leidseplein, one of the tourist squares. Despite the weather and intermittent showers there must have been a hundred or so people milling about. It was not even spring yet and the tourists had started to arrive. Shaven-headed punksters, middle-class families, drugged aged hippies, secretaries on their way to work, some Italian children on a school trip, two nuns and an eponymous figure dressed up as a space creature: no one had to communicate with anyone else and so it became for everyone theater.

Maybe if I gave Sander one of his gifts after the film (the computer game he had wanted) it might cheer him up. If I waited until Saturday, amidst all the melee of the party it would simply be another gift in another box added to the pile. He might not open it when I was there, and if he did there would still be twenty people around and I would have to recede into the background for propriety's sake. His mother: "Oh that was too generous of you." Her neighbor: "Who gave that to you Sander? Oh, is he a friend of your mother's?" I didn't want to think of all the meanings society attached to a non-family, single man giving a boy who was his 'friend' a gift, the fears and suspicions it could raise. Gift giving was one of the most common things in the world, and I did not want to have to think about how uncommon people could make it. To show him that I cared? To manipulate or control? Just enjoy the afternoon!

In the film Michiel sat on my left and Sander on my right. Michiel was unusually friendly, leaning towards me in the film and whispering to me intimately. Sander slumped in his seat and even rested his head on my arm. I held his hand for a time, he seemed so vulnerable.

5. Sander's Dilemma

The manic violence of the film, by a Dutch director gone Hollywood, had been a bit contagious for the boys. As we were walking back to my apartment the two of them were sparring with each other and being a bit too loud and rowdy, Sander gone from depressed to manic. I was starting to feel a little ill, develop a headache; I told them several times to tone it down. Michiel could not stay for dinner and we waited with him at the tram stop until his tram came.

Michiel's departure did not seem to calm Sander down. Niek knew the director of the film casually, and had done some portraits of him a few years back. Sander babbled on about meeting him, going to the US and being in the movies. The film's cold, humanly detached mannerist style was everything I detested most about the modern fantasy action film. But Sander was so enthusiastic and lively, jumping around and imitating some of the stunts in a clumsy, charming, if obnoxious way, that I didn't have the heart to give him a moral lecture and take the risk of plunging him back into depression. At one point he did ask me if I'd liked the film and I said quite honestly that I hadn't. He ignored the remark.

When we got back to the apartment the phone machine's red light was blinking six messages. I rewound the tape. The cat had been sniffing by the front door and Sander had picked him up and was carrying him around the house talking to him. I heard him say, "No you can't go outside. It's too cold and rainy for pussy cats and anyway those street cats are all rough and don't have food and you're a very lucky cat." Soefi did not let everyone carry him. His pale grey lilac point, long aquiline face somehow complemented Sander's. He looked up quizzically and Sander kissed him on the top of the head. I pressed the Play button. My Dutch publisher, Marijke, Niek (which was unusual), my mother, Toon, Erich. I would call Marijke back first.

Sander was in the kitchen. I heard the refrigerator door open. "Feed the cat," I shouted. I went in. "Your mother left a phone message. Do you want to eat here, go out to eat, or eat home."

"What is there?"

"Pasta or meat loaf." I looked in the refrigerator. "Salad, and ice cream for dessert."

"Pasta." He opened the can of cat food, the cat circling his legs, put it down on the floor and went into the study to play a computer game.

I phoned Marijke. She answered after several rings and asked how the film was.

"Sander loved it and I hated it." The words were hardly out of my mouth when I realized I had given her one of her little openings. Now why did I do that? She never resisted them either.

"You don't have to see this garbage with him, you know. And anyway, I'm not sure I want him to see this kind of film. He gets too wild afterwards."

"He's all right, just playing a computer game. It wasn't too bad."

"They're not that good for him. He should have better taste."

"Well, Michiel met us there too, as it turned out, so probably Sander would have wanted to see it anyway. Some of the film was good though. It wasn't any more violent than some of his comic books. I mean it was well made. It didn't seem like the work of someone Dutch though. Very American, you know — gratuitous."

"Niek did a portrait of the director. Not one of his best. Maybe it was the subject. I never liked him very much; he's greedy, and they say he's made millions from this film."

"Yes. It's very successful."

"By the way, I spoke to Niek today and he's going to call you."

"He left a message on my machine right after yours. I'll call him back. What does he want?"

"Some gallery business or other, I think."

"I'll call him back now."

Sander wandered into the living room playing with his GameBoy. It made funny little squeaks and clicks. I asked, "Can Sander stay for dinner or do you want him home? Maybe you'd like to come over too. I was going to make some pasta." She wanted to finish a watercolor. Sander could stay. She wanted him home no later than nine.

I hung up and phoned Toon first instead of Niek. He answered on the first ring, his voice far too loud, no doubt in another of his moods. According to him a meeting with his lawyer today had not gone too well. Some of their expert witnesses would not appear, especially a gallery owner I knew slightly. Could I suggest someone else? I would have to give it some thought.

It was too late to call my Dutch publisher. I wondered what Niek wanted but dialed Dr Born instead. There was no answer. I heard the shower, Sander humming. I was beginning to feel anxious and even more out of sorts, in fact a bit dizzy. Clouds of steam poured out of the bathroom.

I phoned Niek. He wanted to get together with me as soon as possible and would be in the city Thursday. He had 'a proposal to make'. I told him I had an appointment that day, and we arranged to meet on Saturday instead before the party.

"What's it all about?" I asked.

"Just your future, my future and the future of the gallery," he said in a pompous, slurred, overly dramatic way.

The shower stopped and I heard the rings slide back along the chrome shower-curtain rod. Should I put Sander on the line? Niek seemed in a hurry to get off the phone, but I said, "Sander's here. Do you want to talk to him?"

"Well," he hesitated, "put him on for a moment."

I called him and he came wandering into the living room

31

with a large, white cotton towel wrapped around his waist, drooping to his ankles. There were beads of water along his chest, dripping from his hair. He left wet footprints along the carpet. I held out the receiver and went into the kitchen to start dinner but heard him say, "No, I'm doing all right. I got an almost perfect score on the test." A pause, then, "We went to a movie... I didn't have any school today... teachers' meeting or something."

As I bent to take the kettle out of the bottom cupboard I felt quite dizzy and had to hold on to the cabinet door to steady myself. I stood back up slowly. Now what was this all about? My head was swimming and I felt a bit nauseous. I turned around. Sander stood in the doorway. I had not even heard him hang up. He looked at me strangely. I was holding on to the refrigerator door and could feel the blood drain from my face. I closed my eyes, and shook my head to clear it, felt a sharp stab of a headache.

"Boy, you're white." He seemed alarmed. I smiled wanly.

"I feel a bit dizzy. Must be a cold coming on," I said, and closed the refrigerator door. "You're going to catch a cold too if you don't get dressed."

"It's warm in here. You look really weird."

I felt a chill run through me. "I just need something to eat. The pasta won't take long."

He went to the cupboard and took out the big pasta kettle. "I can cook. You should go lie down. I can make pasta; and the sauce," he said. He was filling up the kettle at the sink, his bare shoulders hunched a bit, tensed, muscled. I thought I would let him, and perhaps even stretch out for a minute. I lay down on the couch and Sander came in after a few minutes and sat on the edge next to me. He seemed to be getting back into his mood again. He was playing on his GameBoy and I asked him to turn off the sound. The house was filling with smells, from the sauce, from Sander and coconut shampoo. The golden hair along the top of his back swirled into a spiral at the base of his neck. The towel had parted, his right leg exposed, still a bit brown from summer, child's hair along his calf, the thigh smooth, and muscled from so much biking.

I said, "You're upset about something or other today. You've been acting kind of on edge and a little depressed and when we met Michiel you even crossed to my other side as if you were avoiding him a little. So, is everything all right?"

He shrugged.

"Did you two have an argument?"

He shook his head.

"Well, with someone else at school then." I said it as a matter of plain fact.

He turned to glance at me, then threw his GameBoy on the coffee table. It slid across and onto the floor. He said animatedly, "Yesterday, you know, we were on our way to Zuiderbad to go swimming, the whole class and one of those guys says real loud in front of everyone, 'Heh, Sander, I saw your father with some strange-looking woman last night coming out of a bar and boy were they both drunk'."

I pushed myself upright. Niek must have been with Loo, his Chinese mistress. "So, how did you feel when he said that?"

"I wanted to bash him in the face."

"Did you?"

"No."

"Did you answer back?"

"No! How could I? We were on a tram with lots of people around and our teacher was watching."

"It was a pretty dumb thing to say. It must have hurt your feelings. It was probably better not to answer."

"He's a jerk. I don't want to go to that school any more. They're all jerks."

"Well, Michiel is still your friend."

"He was standing right there and didn't say anything."

"So, you're mad at him too. The two of you were getting along all right today."

"Not really."

He was right of course. "Do you think he had to say anything?"

"He says he's my best friend, doesn't he?"

"Then you should talk to him. Maybe to the other boy

too."

"It won't make any difference."

What he probably meant was that his father would still continue to drink, and it would still continue to be a source of embarrassment to him. I added, "You shouldn't just give up on Michiel. That's not fair. Sometimes it does help to talk about something."

He replied, "What's the sense?" and then suddenly said, "When you go back to San Francisco, will you take me with you? I don't want to stay here anymore. It's a creep place. Take me with you. They have good schools there. You told me they did. I can go to school there. I can talk good English. We could live together. You see, I can cook."

He was obviously pretty upset. I put my arms around him. I said, "You're really upset. I'm sorry you're so upset."

He broke away from me and, springing up from the sofa, went into the kitchen and started banging dishes around. I had not said what he wanted to hear. Beads of sweat had erupted on my forehead. I felt I was making a mess of things. After all, I knew what he wanted me to say, something like, "Sure you can come and live with me; we'll leave tomorrow and life will be perfect." Not that that would ever happen, or that he even meant that it should ever happen. He wanted reassurance. I went into the kitchen and I said to him, "I don't want you to worry. We can always work things out."

It was not until after he had left around seven-thirty, still grumpy and disconsolate, that I had a chance to think it over. I telephoned Erich and explained what had happened. What did Erich think? Did he think that Sander thought I was rejecting him? Here he was suddenly saying he wanted to live with me and I had given him this measured, reasonable, adult answer. I could have said any of a number of positive things, and held out a little hope. Was I that ambivalent? I babbled away into the telephone.

When Erich listened hard he paused before each answer. "I don't understand one thing," he said. "Apparently you're not feeling too well right now but I don't understand why you didn't simply say, 'I love you Sander.' Sometimes that is all a person needs."

"I don't know. I didn't think of it. I do love Sander. I don't know. Maybe it's Toon's trial on Friday or maybe I'm more worried about going back to San Francisco than I thought I was."

"Well, don't be too harsh on yourself. That's not why I'm asking. What I'm wondering about is why you keep wanting some reassurance from Sander of his feelings for you and now, when he says he wants to run away with you and live with you, you don't know how to respond. For Sander, for any boy his age, that's a pretty big thing you know. It must have taken a lot for him to say it. I suppose you're even still wondering if he loves you or not!"

I groaned and had to admit that it was true. I almost said that I didn't know anything about boys anymore, but I said instead, "It's a long time since I've been twelve."

"My God. You're not that old. Thirty-two? Thirty-four? You're impossible. You won't even allow yourself to be a little glad that Sander made that request. Maybe that's the puritan American speaking? Or your Catholic upbringing, or something. Frankly it puzzles me."

"It's just that what Sander was really saying was that he wants to get away from his family problems, run away from his father, maybe his own confusion right now."

The telephone crackled. "You are impossible! Is that all you really think he meant about going to San Francisco? I mean, when was love anything except a confusion of motives and here you are trying to be... trying to... well, reduce it to some cliché about boys. To say the least. What do you expect from him, some kind of pure undistilled kind of ideal love with no other motivation in it except pure love itself! He's going through a lot right now. I think I know what you're thinking though."

Oh my God, I thought, he's about to do to me what I had done with Sander earlier — pretend to read my thoughts while making an educated guess. He said, "I think you're feeling guilty. I think you think that Sander's family problems have made him dependent on you and you're afraid of taking advantage of him. That's why you held back tonight when he said he wanted to live with you."

I burst out suddenly. "Well isn't it? Sentimental, I mean. I know I'm not taking advantage of him, but I simply won't be sentimental about Sander."

"What does it mean to you... I mean, what do you visualize when you hear this awful word? What associations do you have?"

I groaned. I wanted to say, "My God! Always the good therapist!" But I knew that would hurt his feelings. He was trying to draw me out. I bit my tongue and went along with it. "Well... sentimental. What do I visualize? A slippery slope. Sliding down into some morass. Getting caught in something that suffocates you."

"In other words, something you have to stay out of to survive."

"No, not exactly. It's more something that I have to keep the relationship out of for it to survive. It's my responsibility. The way I protect Sander. I have to keep it... real."

There was a pause. "Yes, but look at your reactions right now. You're so worried about being judged for having Sander dependent on you because of his family problems that you can't even bring any sentiment into moments with him. Here's the hard question: do you think Sander would still be in this relationship with you if his parents had not just separated? I remember when I was doing my research..."

I groaned inwardly. He was going to lecture me again.

When he had done his research, he was quick to remind me, he had interviewed about two thousand men who as children had had sexual relationships with adults, and a majority later viewed those relationships as positive. But that was not the point he was trying to make. More than half the boys in these relationships had severe family problems, but a large percentage did not have those family problems, and they still sought relationships with men outside their families for a whole host of reasons. He remembered that one boy had given as his main reason for the friendship the fact that his family was boring and that he and his friend went nice places together. Some had actually said that they liked the sex, which no one wanted to admit.

Erich concluded, "Anyway, the point is that there are a host of reasons for Sander being friends with you, aren't there? You're an American and that's a little exotic for him, and it holds out the promise that through you he can see other countries, other cities — New York, San Francisco. You pay undivided attention to him, which you would under any circumstance, not just the present, because you're crazy about him. Boys love that. Anyone does who has even an ounce of healthy narcissism in their personalities. You take him to action films, swimming, biking in the country, give him massages, breakfast in bed, spoil him a bit. He can tell you anything. Sometimes you stay up talking until late. You tell him stories and understand his school problems. He shares them with you. He tells you about his friends, and when he has trouble with one of them comes to you. You give him a lot of affection because he's so attractive to you. You're what we call in Dutch a *knuffelvriend*, a 'cuddle-friend', like a teddy bear or something. He likes to hug. You tell him he's beautiful at an age when even the slightest blemish can convince a boy that he's some kind of lizard. You teach him things his parents don't take the time for: give him sips of wine, look at photographs with him. You said the other day you were building a model ship together... But you! You concentrate on the problems. And I'm not even mentioning much of your side of all of this and why you want the relationship."

I said, partly in my own defense, "He's very nice to me. He calls me every day he doesn't see me. I like the way when he's with me he babbles on and on. I love boy chatter more than anything. It seems to me to be one of the most wonderful things in the world. Once I was walking with Sander, this was about a year ago, he was holding my hand and chattering away as fast as he could about anything that came into his head. Blah blah blah blah blah, this and that. I really loved him at that moment..." I stopped myself deliberately and said with what I hoped would be understood as quiet humor, "You see, before I know it, I'll be getting all soft and sentimental."

Erich laughed. "Yes, you will." But he hadn't quite finished, although I thought he had certainly made his point. "Let me ask you something. It's a hard question. Please don't be offended." He paused, then asked, "Do you really think that if Sander was from a perfect home you would not be in love with him? In other words is the only thing you love about Sander his dependency on you because of his problems?"

I started to protest that there were a thousand things I loved about Sander, as I was just trying to say. But Erich interrupted again.

"Now let me ask you an even more difficult question. Do you honestly think that if Sander had no family problems at all, that Niek was not an alcoholic, and did not have a mistress, and was not living separate from his mother, that Sander would not in a million years be friends with you? Is that all you have to offer Sander, and is that all you think he wants?"

I did not say anything at all. There was not much to say. After a rather awkward silence Erich added, "Sander is more resilient than you give him credit for."

Part Two: Reminiscences

1. Wednesday Morning, February 28th

I had odd dreams last night, and awakened today with a fever. In one I was standing at a deserted border crossing in the middle of unfamiliar countryside. Roads went off in all directions, spokes from a wheel. A dour, armed soldier with a machine-gun laid across his arms blocked the road. He was dressed in a funny tricornered hat and uniform with epaulettes resembling the Spanish civil guard's that I had seen in photographs by Carel Blazer while doing my research on Monday. He handed me back my passport and said threateningly, "Move on!" I was confused and panicked. Where was I going? What was I doing there? The guard aimed his gun at me.

I awoke in a sweat, sitting bolt upright in bed, and felt my forehead; a slight fever for sure, dizziness, nausea. It was cold in the room. Soefi, buried beneath the covers, thinking I was rising, burrowed his way out, shook his head, yawned. It was only five-thirty. I was shivering and sank back down onto the pillow, coaxing him under the blanket again.

I had another dream. A bronzed Sander was standing nude in the sand dunes, wearing only a wide-brimmed straw hat. A golden, sparkling light as if filtered through dew, surrounded him. He held out his arms, beckoning, and I walked towards him feeling happy and awed.

It was the doorbell that awakened me this time, reluctantly. It was nine-thirty. I struggled into a bathrobe and pressed the intercom. *"Postbode met een aangetekende brief."* My God, Dutch! The postman with a registered letter. I went to the door, still shivering. Rain. Rain and wind again. An official-looking letter with the embossed University seal. I signed for it, closed the door, and threw the unopened envelope on the dining-room table, fed the cat his breakfast, and tried to go back to bed, but the dreams and the letter weighed on my mind and made me restless and I finally retrieved the envelope and tore it open: the Dean wanted me to contact her immediately. The tiered, semi-circular darkened lecture hall where I taught flashed before me: clumps of my hundred-plus students scattered here and there in the vast hollow room; a projector flashing on a white screen desperate social images by Jacob Riis and Lewis Hine, suffering crystallized out of beams of dusty light. I would say to the assembled faces, "Nothing has changed". The Dean was angry. She had been leaving 'transatlantic' messages on my phone machine and I had not contacted her. Should I phone today? I looked at my calendar. I had marked this down as a work day at the library, but I did not feel much like being responsible. I made myself some tea, tried to read, and finally decided to straighten out my cupboards, sort through things and clean up a bit. I dumped everything I could find on the dining-room table and turned on some music. The apartment was quiet. Sander, in school, would not phone me until tonight.

In reading through some of my papers this morning I was struck by how much the events of August actually started in March, and how those of August continue and color now. I had never stopped to think much of the origin of a decision, or even an event that seems to come upon us by surprise. Might they have a natural sequence and logic, flowing one out from the other?

There was a setting, or better, a set, as in 'film' or 'stage'. I had been in Amsterdam several months, by then quite involved in the life of the gallery, there nearly every day for a while preparing for the opening of one of my curated shows, which also meant seeing more and more of Sander. Niek was away, at a photo festival in the United States. He was planning to travel there for two or three months, seeing collectors and dealers about his work, and intending to start an ambitious photo project on the New York subways; it also seemed to me this trip was a trial separation. As it turned out, I was, unfortunately, right. When he returned in June he moved to the farm. Marijke was confiding in me more, but she was also more absorbed in her painting, perhaps as an antidote to the impending break-up. I saw more of Sander.

And so, I take from the cupboard the large cardboard box containing the detritus of my accumulated papers of the last year or two, spilling them out on the bed: diaries and copies of letters, notes and little messages from Sander, photographs of him, of me, of Marijke; little drawings of hers, scraps of papers with lines of poems, simple, one-paragraph thoughts, about my life here, about Sander, about me, about trying to make some sense of him and us, find a semblance of order in it, Sander alone, Sander at the beach, in his living room, in my apartment the first time they came to dine, Sander that first summer seductively stretched on a blanket in the sand dunes, propped up on one elbow, smiling, a towel draped loosely over his hips... Sander twelve recedes to Sander at eleven... March this year to March, April, July, August, the year before...

2. March, Last Year

March 2nd.
Out for dinner at an Italian restaurant with the gallery crowd last night, Sander sat next to me. When it came time to order he said, "I want everything you want." I ordered spaghetti — so did he; a salad, cola, even a cup of tea with a little milk which he does not usually drink. I asked him why he was imitating me and he said, "It's a mirror game."

Today, riding with him on a very crowded tram to the gallery, I sit on one of the single seats and he slides onto my lap, his arm draped over my shoulder. Looking out the window, he identifies the buildings for me, but it also is a game because he knows I know them all: this department store, that shop where he bought his expensive running shoes, that nice bookshop where they have a lot of children's books, his favorites being by Annie Schmidt and will I buy him the new one? His cheek is close to mine, sometimes touches. An elderly woman who had been sitting across the aisle from us gets up to leave and says in English, "Your boy is very beautiful." She smiles benevolently. Father and son, she must be thinking, but she says 'boy' not 'son'.

I finish my work early and take him to a four o'clock movie. He practically sits on top of me, presses his leg against mine, links his arm with mine, leans. He whispers, his mouth close to my ear, his warm breath sending shivers through me. I take his hand; he plays with my fingers; I feel happy.

March 6th.
I was walking Sander home today when we saw something dreadful. A motorbike sped down the narrow street, going far too fast; a dog ran out from behind a car to chase it, was struck and as it turned out killed. The young man fell from his bike but did not appear injured. The owner of the dog, a young woman, ran over shrieking. Sander gasped and I looked at him. He was standing stock still, pale as a ghost. I put my arm around him; he was trembling. I asked him if he was all right, but he hugged me and began to cry; I put my arms around him to comfort him.

I remained for dinner. Before he went to bed I read him another Sherlock Holmes story. The book was designed for children, quarto sized and illustrated with line drawings. I held it low, his head propped against my leg, so he could see the page. I smoothed his hair back and he reached up and touched, but did not take my hand. He said, "Do you think she's still sad?" I knew he meant the owner of the dog, and I said I thought she must be.

March 15th.
I have been at Sander's house a little too much. Marijke keeps inviting me. I think she is lonely and feeling threatened because of uncertainties with Niek, and his being away.

I had gone upstairs to read Sander his story, but he still had too much energy to lie in bed quietly and fall gradually into sleep. He was teasing me and making too much noise, making a trampoline of his bed, pouncing on me, squeezing me around my neck and trying to make me fall backwards. I wrested his arms free and, holding him by the wrists, tried to get him off me and pin him down on the bed. He struggled like a fierce cat, even tried to bite me.

Marijke shouted upstairs, "Who's not going to bed?" He became quite quiet but continued to try to fend me off, his lips closed tightly, a determined look furrowing his brow. I let go of his arms. His pajamas were hunching up his body. He immediately tried to tickle me, grabbing at my stomach, my sides. Buttons came, or were, undone, mine, his. I started tickling him instead. He shouted at top volume, "Help! Help! Stop! Stop! Help." I found his bare stomach and scrambled my fingertips over it, but he screamed so loudly I stopped. He was hunched in a ball, looking up at me panting, his face red, and then quite deliberately he stretched out his legs in order, I think, to show me he had an erection, pushing out towards my hand. He put an arm behind his head. I did not know what to do, but suddenly without thinking, I hugged him. Smiling embarrassedly he scrambled beneath the covers.

When I went downstairs Marijke asked what all the noise had been about and I said, "Rough-housing."

March 19th.
Yesterday Marijke said that she wanted to show me a portfolio of photographs that had been left at the gallery which she thought I would like. They were not very good boy nudes, flat, two dimensional, the backgrounds sloppy, the lighting wrong. I was a bit put out because she thought I would like them. Why should I? I felt very uncomfortable about looking at them with her and made some sort of comment like, "Oh, they show some talent, but they're really not that good, certainly not something we would want to bother with." I went away feeling angry, feeling that she had presented me with some sort of test to draw me out about my sexuality.

And then, later, Sander told me that she said he was spending too much time with me, and that he preferred me to her. So, I phoned her today and asked if we could have lunch together. There were, in any case, several things at the gallery we had to go over because Niek was going to be away for several weeks, and I was, if anything, rather angrier with her than she with me. She had been very friendly whenever I'd asked her if Sander could do something with me, and I felt I had been sensitive about asking her first, and then no sooner was he home than she had castigated him for being with me!

Over lunch in the cafe near the gallery I simply brought it up right away, trying to sound as natural as possible. I told her that Sander had mentioned to me what she had said and that this had surprised me. She immediately fumbled for a cigarette, frowning.

"Well," she said, "that's between Sander and me." It was not, she claimed, the fact that Sander was spending time with me, but what he made of it, that bothered her. He was holding me up to her. The other day, for example, he had gotten angry about her 'nagging' him over cleaning up his room, and had said, "Will doesn't nag me or holler at me." He had also threatened to move out and come and live with me if she didn't stop, which I assured her had not been put in his head by me. Did she want me to say something to Sander? She felt she could handle it herself, and then added a remark which made the conversation touchier: "I haven't had any experience with a man making friends with a boy and I suppose it would be foolish not to think it would create problems."

I felt cornered and unsure, and replied, "I certainly would never encourage Sander to play us off against each other. In any case," I added, "I'm not sure Sander is really saying he wants to come to live with me. It sounds more emotional blackmail so he won't have to do his chores. He's probably bluffing."

She suddenly laughed. "I called his bluff. I told him to stop the nonsense and clean up his room."

It suddenly occurred to me that with Niek away, and unlikely to move back with her, she must almost certainly be feeling very vulnerable and needing reassurance.

I said, "I'm afraid I've been spoiling Sander a bit. You know, when he comes to my house for dinner I don't ask him to help with the dishes or pick up after himself. That sort of thing. He can be pretty difficult at times, but I think he loves you and would not really want to move in with me, even if he has a pretty easy time of it around me. Maybe my pampering him goes to his head a little."

"Well, I don't know what goes on when he visits you, but when he comes back home he is harder to handle."

I could feel my face flushing. Nothing much had happened between us. He had stayed over two weekends. He slept on the couch. Don't mix business and pleasure: that was the age-old wisdom, which Dr Born had recently reiterated. I kept silent, and that seemed to make her nervous.

She crushed out her cigarette, looked directly at me. "Of course, I trust you." But she said it so aggressively that I thought it was more a challenge than a statement of fact.

March 24th.
A series of small things between Sander and me:

— We were in my apartment, rolling around on the floor wrestling. I had pushed him against one wall and was trying to fend off his arms to tickle him. He was struggling to free himself. I pinned his hands down on the carpet. He squirmed this way and that. I noticed that his fly was open. "Your fly is open." I said, not letting go of his hands. "So?" he said. I let him go. He got up angrily, and made no move to zip himself up.

— I was reading to him another of the Sherlock Holmes stories, 'The Man with the Twisted Lip'. I opened the book; he nestled against me. I read, "Isa Whitney... was much addicted to opium." I said, "My God, what am I reading to you!" But he won't let me stop. He turns the pages for me, and is looking up at me. He starts playing with my beard and I begin to get aroused. I swallow. He says, "Does that feel good?" I nod and he continues.

— A few days ago he said that one of his classmates had been making fun of a boy before swimming practise because he was wearing 'fag', bikini underpants. It had been apparently the occasion for not just some ribbing but also for some discussion of sexual practices. One boy said that a doctor (witch-doctor?) told him if a man gave you a blow job you became queer. There were a string of old wives' tales: if a man's cum got inside a boy then he had some kind of magic power over you; if you had sex with a girl during her menstrual cycle you could become infected and die; girls were hornier than boys and if you turned them on they couldn't stop and you got sores on your cock; if you masturbated too much it was like losing two pints of blood and you would get thinner and thinner and die.

He was quite solemn about all this. Identity transferences, gender anxieties, performance fears, sex and death, sex and disease, the value of abstinence: all of these superstitions learned at eleven seemed rather sad to me. I tried to explain that a man doing certain things with a boy didn't make the boy into anything, like the magician turning the egg into a chicken we had seen at a carnival. Masturbation was not harmful as long as you didn't do it six times a day, and even then... Some primitive people, in New Guinea, thought a man's sperm had magic power, but this was Holland. I was trying to convince him there was no magic in sex, but of course at his age he wanted to believe that there was. Perhaps I should have looked for examples of the positive magic of sex?

— And, a couple of weeks ago after helping Marijke with the dishes I went upstairs to Sander's room. He was supposedly doing homework but I found him lying on his bed sorting out his rock and shell collection. He knows the scientific name for each piece, from encyclopaedias of rocks and shells I gave him last Christmas, and began showing me the new things his uncle just brought him from Sri Lanka. They are mostly ore samples of semi-previous stones. It takes him a long time to show me everything, perhaps half an hour goes by. I am sitting next to him on the bed. His thin tee-shirt has slid up his back. I have my arm around him affectionately. He pushes away the stones and curls up in a ball against me and I rub his taut back, first through his shirt and then under it. His body is hot, feverishly hot and smells a bit of sweat. He squeezes himself harder and harder against me. I bend over him protectively.

— We are sitting together on the couch. He shows me a card trick. I find it funny and laugh. He looks at me affectionately and suddenly seems embarrassed. He looks down and says quietly, "You're my best friend." I respond: "You're mine too."

March 30th.
Marijke finally blurted it out. "Are you and Sander...?" not actually mouthing the exact words. I said, "No."

She said, "No not yet, or no."

I said, "I like boys if that's what you're asking, but I hate putting a label on myself. It seems so meaningless."

"That's not what I asked."

"Sander is a friend."

"For now?"

"I hope we'll be friends for a long time."

She snapped, "Stop answering around me. In other words, you're not making any promises?"

"I didn't say that." I could feel a few beads of sweat trickle down my side.

"Well then let me be clear. I think Sander is young for his age, and far too young for some kind of complicated emotional friendship. I think he should just enjoy being a boy while he can. There'll be time enough in the future for complications."

"Complications isn't all an adult can offer him in a friendship."

"If it's kept simple."

I knew what she was saying, of course. Sex is complicated, an adult complication. That's the way it is in the modern world. We should not bring adult sexuality into a child's world. If there is going to be sex in a child's world then it should be with other children. Maybe then it has some chance of staying simple, staying part of their play world. An adult could not get back to that sense of sex as play because of its strong emotional connotations in the adult's world. It was an illusion.

I did not know what to say. Everything sounded trite. I

thought of saying something about sex being morally neutral for me, but that was not really true. Or that it was an expression of love for me, not just an act of physical relief, which was true. She no doubt wanted me at that moment to promise not to have sex with Sander. I could not get myself to do that. I was glad we were talking about it, I said. That would have never happened in America. Perhaps we were talking around it. We continued for another half an hour, at the end of which she said she thought it would be better if Sander and I were to see each other less frequently.

March 31th.
I spoke to Erich Born today about the conversation with Marijke. I had written it down right away, so I could quote it more or less verbatim. As I had expected his first remark was to reiterate, "As I said, don't mix business and pleasure. It doesn't turn out well."

I told him some of the incidents that had happened between Sander and me and he laughed. "We are wonderful at reading things into situations. Sander leaves his fly open and you think he wants to be seduced."

"Well?"

"It might be broken. Or he might be forgetful. He might simply want praise for his boyhood. It's dangerous to read meanings into things. I could say, after all, that your stories only show that he is attached to you, that he no doubt has feelings for you."

"I think he's bonding."

"Bonding. Well, that's a new one for me."

I knew it could not be a new one for him but I went on, "Perhaps because his father is away right now and he feels insecure."

"Bonding. Is that the same for you as love?"

"I don't know. I don't think it's the same as symbiosis."

I was thinking of it as something visual: there is an imaginary circle drawn around Sander and at some point the boundary is extended to include me. I am within the boundaries of his self. Does he draw me within? Do I rather intrude into it?

It seems to happen of itself. When you are in his circle you have certain obligations: to put up with his moods, fulfill certain emotional needs. There is something absolute about the circle — you are either inside or out. The bond is bestowed. I am 'dubbed' his friend. I did not say any of this though.

Erich said, "You're taking a considerable risk if it gets pushed further with him."

"Well, if I had an analyst right now he would say building some risk into your life is healthy."

"Well, I doubt a good analyst would apply that directly to this situation. Some risk, but not too much. Anyway, it's good that his mother brought up the topic; and, after all, she didn't forbid you outright from seeing him."

"I feel I was a little too evasive with her. But I got confused."

"I keep forgetting you're American. Talking about something ad nauseam is peculiarly Dutch perhaps. Perhaps being American is your greatest disadvantage. You don't know how to negotiate Dutch personalities, Dutch family situations yet. You have no instincts for it the way we would. But, yes, that might also be your greatest advantage. You might come across as naive but not as a dissembler. The most important thing, as far as I can see is that you don't rationalize Sander to yourself."

Don't rationalize! He has my number, I thought.

3. The Texel Diary: August, Last Summer

Those summer weeks on the island with Sander compact themselves for me into the image from my dream. The house where we were staying was built on the edge of the dunes and at the back of the yard there was a tool shed painted, uncharacteristically, a brilliant white. It was early afternoon and I had been looking for him so that we could bike into town. Around the corner of the shed I found him standing there, nude, wearing only a straw hat. The sun fully illuminated his body, though the hat shaded his face. He did not see me at first, but was not embarrassed when he caught me admiring him. He slipped on his blue running shorts, slipped his feet into his sandals and smiled.

This morning I spent some time looking through books, having some vague recollection that I had seen this image somewhere. And suddenly, there he was, or at least there was the reproduction of an nineteenth-century oil painting by Arthur Lemon of a nude Italian boy, painted on Capri. But it was Texel, and Sander, though I had quite forgotten I had ever seen this image in this book. Even the painting had something of the same happiness and even awe that I had felt from the dream. The painting was quite beautiful, though Lemon's work is quite forgotten now.

August 1st.
Friends have leant Marijke a house on the northern Dutch island of Texel for the month of August, and she has asked me if I want to go and keep her and Sander company. I am hesitating. Niek has returned from his trip to the US but he has moved to the farm in Friesland and there is a lot of tension between them right now. If I go I am afraid that she'll drag me into their separation; that's all I will hear about for three weeks. She has gone from rational ("The marriage wasn't working for a long time, and it was about time we accepted it and went our own ways"), to depression ("I suppose it's as much my fault as his"), to rage ("If it weren't for that bitch he's taken up with now..."). It also might seem to Niek that I was siding with Marijke by being with her. I still have to work with him at the gallery, and think it is better for me not to accompany them. Of course, Sander wants me to go, and being with him is a tempting proposition, though I've been trying for weeks now to keep my involvement under control.

It really is tempting to go. Texel is one of my favorite places: vast tracks of quiet open country and traffic-free back roads, expanses of sheep-grazing meadows, flat lands with a vast expanse of cloud-domed sky. The Dutch say the island is too overrun with German tourists in the summer and tend to stay away, but whenever I have been there I've found the roads relatively empty and the eastern extremity, a dune and bird reserve, at times deserted. The house is apparently in this area, bordering on the reserve, and I keep rationalizing that I can get off by myself and birdwatch, beachcomb, or any of a number of things that I enjoy. Sander is nagging me. He says his mother is painting all the time, and it will be boring for him. I can take my work with me, he says; he would leave me alone. It is only a couple of hours back to the city if I don't like it.

August 8th.
Today was my first day on the island. The ferryboat ride only takes about fifteen minutes but the psychological break with Amsterdam, the 'mainland', seems absolute. I stood on the deck letting the wind blow in my face, blow away the city. It is amazing how different I felt. I had brought my bicycle and hoped that the saddle bags and my knapsack had everything I would need in the way of books, Dutch summer clothes, with the inevitable sweater and rain gear, and the usual array of modern body bric-a-brac: deodorant, hand, lip and sun cream.

Marijke had drawn me a map and when I had biked down the ferryboat ramp I stopped by a food stand to go over the route. I calculated it would take me at least an hour and a half to bike to the other end of the island, to the house marked with an X. It was a sunny day, not much wind. The coast road was lined with scrub pine and smelled fresh. I saw so many birds, pheasants, and rabbits among the trees it made me even more aware of how much I missed nature in the city. Not even the rustle of a single leaf could be heard from my apartment windows.

By the time I was nearing the house I do not think I even felt one ounce of stress. I stopped at a crossroads to check again. On my left was a pine grove, on my right a high hedge behind which I could see a white cottage, and sheep grazing in a pasture. I had passed, a kilometer back, a bungalow park and saw that, and the intersection, marked on my map. I pedalled on: a break in the trees on my left, a dirt road wriggling back into the dunes, and a few hundred feet on, obscured by bushes, a low brick house with forest-green shutters and white wooden gables. The yard was well tended, flowers in profusion, the lawn a brilliant green from the unusually wet July we had just gone through. Marijke's car was not in the drive, Sander's bike was lying on the ground by the door. There was a note pinned to the door, "Shopping, be back around three, help yourself."

I made a cup of coffee and took it outside. I had not given them a definite time of arrival and regretted it a bit. As I had been biking I had imagined Sander running out of the house to greet me. He would throw his arms around my neck and wrap his lithe legs around my waist. Marijke had done a considerable amount of work on the garden; it was weeded, freshly turned and flourishing. The yard did not so much end as blend into dune grass. I found a path at the back half hidden by scrub pine, and followed it a bit until I heard surf. It was entirely deserted, quiet, the high dunes protecting the walker from the worst of the winds. The tops of the trees leaned south, all sheered off at about the same height by winter storms.

I heard the car and went around to the front nearly bumping into Sander, carrying an overloaded blue canvas shopping bag he could only manage with two hands, dragging and lifting, dragging and lifting, perhaps a bit exaggeratedly. They have already been here a couple of weeks and his hair is bleached straw, dry and unkempt, his skin is a fawn brown. He pushed past me sullenly, obviously in a bad mood, grunting hello. Marijke waved. "Don't pay any attention to him," she said, not looking any too cheerful herself. She had made him leave his arcade game before he'd finished.

I helped unload the car. Inside Sander was sulking in a chair. He looks incredibly healthy, a sheen of red burnishing his cheeks. Was he in a bad mood because of the game, I asked. "I could have got a record score," he said. The next time we went to town I'd play him a game, and I bet I would win. The offer did not seem to matter, he merely grunted something indistinguishable.

In fact, he stayed in a bad mood for much of the rest of the afternoon. There was a television but no cable or antenna and as he flicked through the channels not getting anything worth watching a burst of anger flared out. I asked him if he wanted to play checkers; he glowered. Monopoly? He went upstairs to the attic room he had commandeered for his bedroom without answering me.

Marijke usually found a way of dealing with his moodiness, by having him chop the dinner vegetables, run an errand, involve him in what she was doing. She was sitting in the kitchen as sullen as he, smoking too many cigarettes and drinking too much coffee. The kitchen window was open; the air was becoming cold and damp. She did not say much to me and I felt awkward.

I was about to go outside when she asked me if I had talked to Niek before leaving the city. I said I had spoken to him very briefly, and that his US trip seemed to have been successful. She aggressively crushed her cigarette to a pulp in the ashtray, her forehead wrinkled, eyes narrowed and tense. She said that upon his return from Houston he had come by the house once to pick up some clothing, and had then gone directly to the farm.

I took some cola from the refrigerator, poured myself and Sander a glass, and went upstairs to find him. If everyone was in such a terrible state I thought something must have happened. Niek sometimes has a cruel tongue, and there might have been sharp words spoken. I could imagine him intensely plundering the closets and drawers of the Oudeschans house and then walking out overdramatically — not a pleasant thought.

The door to the room where Sander was staying was at the foot of the attic stairs. I stood, cold glass in hand, wondering if I should go up. I didn't hear him, and finally ascended the stairs slowly. The room obviously belonged to the landlord's child: toy airplanes drifted lazily in the draft from the open dormer window; a couple of shelves were loaded with children's books and toys, an old, dirty and rusty looking telescope stood propped in the corner on a shaky tripod. Sander was lying on his side on the bed paging through a comic book, but not reading it. He still looked quite morose. I put the cola down on the nightstand and sat on the edge of the bed. The wind was picking up and a large bank of dark grey clouds was massing. I was trying to find some sort of idea or project to draw him out and my eyes lit on the telescope. I exclaimed enthusiastically over it. We could take it outside tomorrow and clean it up, I suggested, perhaps even bike into the village and see if there was a bookshop and whether it had an astronomy book.

I took the telescope to the window and was surprised that, in spite of its outer appearances, there were no scratches on the powerful lens and it gave a good clear view. I babbled on a bit, about its being a pretty good one, and if it was clear enough tonight we could see quite a lot. He continued to leaf forlornly through his comic book.

God alone knows what has upset him so much, though there is enough going on to guess: a family break-up, his mother and father fighting all the time. Surely he must be afraid. I could hear Marijke moving around downstairs.

August 9th.
Today Sander still seemed not quite himself. Whatever it was that had disturbed him still remains festering at the back of his mind. I was sitting in the kitchen when he came down for breakfast. He stood next to me, puffy-eyed, dazedly pouring cereal and milk into the bowl, glancing at me now and again, gruff, but teasing me a little.

I suggested we take the telescope outside, take it apart and give it a good cleaning, oiling and polishing. I had had a telescope as a child but not such an expensive one. As we began to clean it we found a date, 'Bausch and Lomb, 1919'. I felt thrilled. It had been made in Rochester and I had spent an internship at the photography museum there for two summers when I thought I wanted to be a curator. It gave me something to talk about. The dirt was external and it did not look as if the interior of the lens was disturbed. We labored over it with damp rags, brass cleaner, and oil for the better part of an hour. As a little game I said that we could not look through it until it was completely cleaned, but then he could have the first look. Of course, this meant that he immediately had to have a look, though I kept pushing him away. The physical contact seemed to break the ice a bit. We put it carefully back on the tripod and I twirled the screw tightly into place. I stepped back and with a flourish said, "You first." He bent over, pointing it carefully at a house quite far away at the end of a broad stretch of heath.

"Wow!"

"Well? How does it work?"

"Wow, look at that!"

"Come on, give me a look. Can you see anything? Is it a total bust?"

I nudged him and he yielded his place reluctantly. A house leapt at me over space with incredible clarity. An elderly woman was digging in a flower bed and a cat prowled near her legs.

Later, in the afternoon, we biked over to the middle of the island to the seal reserve station. He wanted me to buy him a stuffed seal for his bed and I broke down and indulged him, even though I knew Marijke would not like my spending money on him. One of the seal cows was sitting quite charmingly up on the lead ledge of the tank wall, a crowd of children gathered all around her. She was very large, longer than a Dutch adult, heavy with fat and perhaps a baby. She did not seem at all disturbed, her whiskered face turned this way and that, smelling and basking in the sun and attention. Her tail rose and shuddered, settled, rose and shuddered. Sander sat near and slowly edged his way until he was almost next to her. She allowed this, and the liberty of his gingerly extending his hand to touch her head. I stood back several paces watching, and was not sure if Sander or the seal delighted me more.

He seems to have completely forgotten his sullenness. Perhaps it is only animal magic. Sander, eleven — filled with enthusiasm and himself. The seal cow permitting him to touch her had bestowed a certain special worth on him. He glowed with life.

August 10th.
Sander has been growing a lock of hair at the back of his neck for several weeks. It is very popular right now with some friends his age. I am not sure what significance it is supposed to hold for him; he says that it's 'cool'. So far he does not have the single ear stud in his right ear some of his schoolfriends have. Marijke has forbidden it. The stud seems to signify to the boys themselves something macho, perhaps signals something a bit sexually daring to the girls in their class. The thought of piercing his ear frightens him a bit, which Marijke, telling him that he can get an infection, does not try to dispel. That ends the discussion for a time, though the tail, which she does not like either, has gotten longer and longer. I measured it a week or two ago. It was nearly three inches — light brown, gold-flecked filaments thin as spider's woof; it curls at the end and refuses to hang straight.

He came wandering into the living room today to find me, sat down on the sofa next to me where I had been reading, and handed me a pair of scissors. He wanted the lock cut off. He turned his back, waiting. He was wearing a white sleeveless tee-shirt and blue nylon running shorts. I took the hair in my hand and pulled it a little, looking around his cheek to get his attention, and asked him why he wanted me to cut it off. He has been so defensive about it I thought perhaps he needed reassurance again, so I told him, perhaps for the tenth time, that I liked it, that I thought it made him look sexy. He turned to look at me, his hazel eyes narrowed and sharp with determination. "I don't want it anymore."

"Well, okay then, I'll cut it off, but first tell me why," I insisted tugging at it a little affectionately.

"Because."

"Because." I said. I threw the scissors on the couch in mock disgust, wondering if he was going to get stubborn on me again, keep it all to himself, or — what was worse — expect me to divine his hidden thoughts as if I had had some godly power bestowed on me by adulthood, or our friendship. I held on to the lock though, pulling it gently. He was looking directly at me, and my arm was curled around him. Perhaps his friend, Michiel, had made a remark? They were always teasing each other about gender things: who was stronger, who could win at arm wrestling, who a certain girl in his class liked better. But he had not seen Michiel for a couple of weeks and would hardly have harbored a remark that long. I didn't think that could be it, but I thought it was a good place to start.

"I suppose Michiel has been saying you look like a girl or something?" Our faces were quite close. I felt his breath against my cheek. He turned away, not meaning to remove my hand though, and leaned back against me. I put my other arm around his shoulder.

I thought of Michiel: brown skin, half Indonesian, half Dutch, green eyes, his black hair quite long, almost on his shoulders. When Sander had started growing his tail I thought it was a kind of rivalry-of-attractiveness with Michiel.

"Michiel's hair is pretty long, and anyway you aren't usually bothered that much by him."

He said in a rather whiny and none too sincere way, "I don't want it any more. It looks stupid."

"Who says?"

"She said I did everything my friends did, that I was becoming a conformist and had no character and it made me look like a freak."

She was obviously Marijke, and the remark must have been what had made him sulk.

"So?"

"So, just cut it off."

I was on thin ice. I did not want to contradict Marijke, or take his side against her. "What do you want?"

"I don't know."

"Do you like it? Do you want to keep it? Do you want to cut it off? What?"

"Everyone's growing one."

"Well, that's not a good reason, but your wanting it is a good reason."

He got abruptly and said, "She's a jerk."

I said, "Oh come now, she's just under a lot of strain. Anyway, you don't have to get into such a fuss about it. I have an idea. If you still want to cut it off tomorrow I'll cut it off and I promise not to say one word even." I picked up the scissors and snip-snipped with them in the air. "Snip, snip, not a word, and besides we said we were going biking to town for an ice cream."

August 12th.
Sander's moodiness returns now and again like some sharp, annoying muscle twinge. Marijke continues morose, defensive, a bit too sharp with Sander; she spends most of her time in the attic studio or outside in the landscape working on her watercolors for the fall exhibition, though there have been a couple of evenings where we played games together in the kitchen. I brought some work with me, the draft of a chapter of my book, and naively set myself the goal of finishing it in the ten days I planned to be here. It is hard to concentrate with the atmosphere in the house so heavy. I haven't brought the right books either from Amsterdam, and have been thinking of going back, even if only for a day or so.

I sat in the kitchen this morning talking to her for a while. She is in a quandary. Her gallery director, Cees, phoned last night and wants her to go down to Amsterdam to see him. He has had a cancellation and wants to put her in the September slot, which is little more than a month away. It has made her angry, which I can't quite follow, and has sent her into a panic: she has no confidence at all in her work; she isn't ready for a show; she doesn't have enough good material for an exhibition. She knows what I think already, that her work is fresh and innovative: impressionistic, psychological, figurative in a dramatic way as if she were trying to cram a whole novel into one scene. Last night she showed me her latest work and I especially liked it. It is titled, ironically, 'The Conversation', and depicts three nudes — man, woman, and young boy — all with their backs to each other at corners of the picture, the center occupied by a bare green kitchen table. It is stark and effective, reminds me of the American impressionist Thomas Dewing, or perhaps the neo-realist Pedersen-Krag.

"I'm not ready for a show," she said. "Maybe late November, but not right now."

I knew he could be pushy. She had complained about him before. He had been very insistent on the phone, and she had promised to phone him back today.

"He's bullying me; he's only giving me a show out of friendship with Niek, or because of my grandfather."

I told her this was nonsense, that after all shows cost galleries lots of money and business was business. I was sure the director believed in her work. She was completely confused, and I finally suggested she invite him here: after all the new work was here; she couldn't possibly transport it all to Amsterdam; he might like to get away from the city for a day or two; I wouldn't mind sleeping on the couch if she invited him to stay over.

She said, "You don't know Cees. He's an old-fashioned Dutch male. If I say come here he'll get arrogant and tell me how busy he is. He can be insufferable."

"Well. You can be firm, play the role of the artist devoted to her art, of being in the superior position to the gallery director. That's what our photographers do all the time." I added, rather piously, "You have to believe in yourself more. You're an incredibly good artist and it's to his advantage to show you and have your work. I'm repeating myself, but I say stand firm."

That did not seem to cut so fine an impression, but she did telephone him back an hour or two later. I overheard her side and as far as I could tell at first he said no he could not leave the city, that was absolutely impossible. Well, the work was here, she said, and that was that. She wasn't going to carry it back to Amsterdam, and he should see it in its setting. There was a pause. Well, yes, she said, if he came in the next few days there would be enough to see. Yes, she could take out time from working. Yes, there were ferries more or less every hour on the half hour, and there were a lot of guest-houses nearby and she knew the people who owned one of them and would make a reservation for him. Yes, the day after tomorrow would be fine. The two-thirty ferry was perfect.

This morning when I went downstairs at seven she was all in a state about Cees's arrival. She had obviously been up quite early. There were already three cigarette butts in the ashtray and the coffee pot was half empty.

It was nearly noon before Sander was up. I was working at my laptop computer and beginning to feel hungry when I heard hammering coming from out behind the house. I poked my head out the bathroom window and saw that he was making a lop-sided bird house, the roof all crooked and gaping. I shouted down to him, and said I would be out in a minute, having promised to bike into town with him to buy him some shells or rocks for his collection at a shop we had seen but not been in a few days before. Marijke was meeting Cees and either taking him here or going out for coffee first; she was not sure. I asked her if it was all right if Sander and I went a bit later into town and ate a pizza out and saw a film. It would be still quite light at nine o'clock when we would be biking home. The weather was quite fine.

The town was hectic. A flea market had attracted every vacationer and inhabitant on the island, it seemed. We left our bikes in the village square and it took us half an hour to wend our way through the displays of local cheese and wool products, food vendors, street musicians, jugglers, and sightseers. When we finally managed to reach the shop just before six it was closed. Sander seemed intimidated by the crowds. He held on to my hand and stayed close by my side.

At the pizza restaurant the waitress forgot to take the orders for our drinks and returned to ask whether or not 'my son' wanted a coke. The restaurant was gaudy, with passable food that was a grade more authentic than the decor: empty chianti bottles, fish nets and plastic green grapes hanging from the ceiling, an Italian's idea of what a non-Italian thought authentic Italian should be. It did not work.

Sander was playing with his salad. He was in his not-liking-greens phase. I said, "Listen here, son, don"t play with your food."

He pretended to pout, but managed a smile. "You're not my mother," he said, emphasizing 'mother'.

"She still bothering you about your tail?" He shrugged again and I said, trying to draw him out, "If I were you... God forbid!... but if I were you I'd be pretty upset and angry about all that's happening right now with your father moving out and your mother being in a bad mood so much. I guess, well, maybe it would make me pretty moody and I wouldn't want to talk about any of it too much."

He exclaimed, "He's a real jerk."

Of course, he meant Niek. "Why?"

"You don't know what he said to me."

"Was it that bad?"

"Yes."

"Well?"

"Promise not to tell."

"Of course I promise not to tell." I tried to sound offended.

"He said why didn't I go to live with him in Friesland, in the middle of nowhere. You know, leave the city and go up there with him. He's a creep."

"What's so bad about that?"

"You don't get it. He's lying. He doesn't care about me. He just wants to go live with him to get me away from my mother. He doesn't really care."

I was a bit puzzled. "You really think he wants you to choose between him and your mother?"

He became quite angry. "It's a game. That's wrong. He wants me to do the wrong thing. He's a fucking drunk. I hate him." He had raised his voice and now became embarrassed, glanced around to see if anyone had heard his outburst, and lowered his head. His face was flushed with emotion; he bit his lip.

"What did you say when he said that. I mean, did you at

least tell him you didn't want to go and live with him?"

"No. He doesn't listen to me. He never listens. He said it was better for me in the country, away from the city. You know, healthier air and that crap. Pretending it was good for me. I hate Friesland. The wind blows all the time and when it rains you can't even go to a movie. There's nothing to do. And he'd just go out with her to a restaurant or somewhere without me and then I'd be left alone at home with that stupid dog, and the wind blowing."

Suddenly, as if sharply exhaled, energy seemed to drain from his voice. He poked at his food with his fork, but did not eat. He said quietly, "Anyway, he just wants to use me. Doesn't care what I. Not really." He looked up at me. I thought for sure that he was going to start crying; his eyes were red. He added, hardly able to get his words out, "Don't you see, he's evil."

I was taken aback not just by the remark but by the emotion behind it. I said passionately, "Oh Sander, You don't have to go anywhere with him. You have a choice. You can stay in Amsterdam. It's not all that bad. You can tell him clearly that's what you want."

He bit his lip; for a moment a look of real fear passed over his face. "He won't listen even if I say that. He'll try to make me go. You don't know him. He doesn't listen. He'll force me."

I thought it might be time to lighten things a bit, and said, "Well, if he tries to do that I'll beat him up. After all, there's lots of people around and what is he going to do, kidnap you or something? We won't let him do that... I mean, what do you imagine? He's going to come in the middle of the night and steal you or something?"

He said, "You don't know him like I do." He looked at me, clearly feeling threatened. Niek had a temper but I knew for a fact that he had never struck Sander even once. The point though was that Sander's imagination was his reality at this moment, so I pressed on. "So, what's he going to do, tie you up and drag you there? What do you imagine? Sneaking into your bedroom like some robber and carrying you away."

He shook his head vigorously raising his fist, "He wouldn't dare."

"He certainly wouldn't," I affirmed. "You have some choice too. It's clear, isn't it? You want to stay with your mother, and I'm sure she'll want that too, so, he would have a big fight on his hands if he wanted to force you to do anything. Have you talked to your mother about it?" He shook his head. "Well, maybe you should talk it over with her too." Almost as an afterthought I added, "I don't think your father would do anything stupid. He loves you..."

Sander interrupted me. "No," he said. "If he really loved me he wouldn't be asking me like this at all."

I could think of nothing to say. A harsh truth had surfaced for which at that moment I could find no reply.

After the meal we went to a film at the little local movie theater. It was extremely crowded and we had to sit in a back row against the side wall. Sander was obviously distracted and did not laugh much at the inane American comedy the rest of the audience seemed to enjoy. He played with the fabric on the seat arm, twisted, slumped and slid this way and that, but when I asked him if he wanted to leave he shook his head. I don't think he saw much of the film, but he did not want to go back to the house either.

I had promised him an ice cream afterwards and hoped it would lighten his mood a little. He still seemed so disturbed. It was about nine-thirty and I phoned Marijke from a green phone booth in the village square to say we were heading back shortly and would be there in half an hour or so. There was still, because of the northern latitude, a good deal of light. Our bikes were locked by the side of the churchyard and we went through a stone gate to sit down and finish our cones. The church had been recently, impeccably restored: the seventeenth-century brick repointed. It was simple and elegant, modestly showing its great refinement, a very Dutch trait. There was no one in the churchyard at that hour. It was very quiet. We sat together on the back steps of the church, facing tall elms and rustling poplars. Sander did not say anything. He did not want to finish his ice cream and I took it from him and threw it in a nearby waste bin. I sat down next to him again.

I put my arm around his shoulder. "I'm sorry you're so upset. But it'll be all right you know."

He leaned against me, a shudder trembling his body. I squeezed his shoulder reassuringly. "You'll see. It'll all calm down and you'll feel better."

"They'll never be married again." He looked up at me, intensely pained.

"No. I don't think they will. I wish I could tell you they would. But you can see both of them, you know, and work it out somehow."

He bit his lip and his eyes filled. I said, "Oh, Sander, I'm so sorry. But I'll stand by you. I'll be your friend. I'll try not to let you down." I held him with both arms now, pressing my cheek against his hair. I heard him, through sniffles and gasps say almost inaudibly, "You're my best friend."

I felt breathless. I squeezed him and said in Dutch, *"Oh Sander, ik hou van je...* I love you."

"I know you do," he said.

I rummaged awkwardly in my pocket and managed to extract my handkerchief. He stopped crying. I did not want to leave the village, and found the long bike ride back to the house very difficult. Thank God Marijke was not downstairs when we arrived, but in the studio. I asked Sander if he wanted some tea, but he went straight to his room. I looked in on him a couple of hours later and he was sleeping, it seemed, peacefully.

4. The Texel Diary: Sand Dunes and Sander

August 15th.
It is nearly midnight and the house is quiet. I have been sitting for a long while by the open window enjoying the soft Dutch night, cool but not cold, not too much wind, the sound of night birds but no cars, no planes flying overhead, and sand dunes hiding the sound of surf. Nothing threatens, no

danger from break-ins, no unwanted intruders, nor a nature that might overturn the gentle tranquility, submerged in the smell of scrub pine and damp earth.

Cees has come and gone and the arrangements finally worked out for Marijke's exhibition. He decided on a retrospective to include the last five years of work, a 'long-deserved launching of her career' as he put it, and to my surprise she has accepted this calmly. They agreed that the opening should be in November so they could properly prepare for it.

I had promised Marijke to entertain Sander today while Cees came over to look at the work, discuss contracts and the like. I tried to think of something special to do with him and about noon went in to wake him up. He had pulled the top of his sleeping-bag over his head, and was huddled down in it. When I tried to peel it back and get him up he was holding it in so tight a grip that I could barely get it away. It's already noon, I told him; he had to get up. When he still didn't move I managed to get an arm free with which to drag him out. He was by now laughing, though struggling, and finally, with mock defiance he said, "All right. Let me go. I'll get up then!" He pushed the sleeping-bag down and threw a smelly sock at me; I made a fuss about it being dirty and I didn't want such a thing in my face and he threw the other. I grabbed him and tickled him and he shrieked. I stopped. Marijke was painting upstairs, and I told him to be quiet. "Then leave me alone," he said, pulling on his shorts, reaching inside matter-of-factly to adjust himself before zipping them up. I asked him what he wanted to do today: go back to the seal reserve, bike again into town? It was a beautiful day and I suggested we take the telescope out to the dunes and have a picnic, play pirates or something. While he ate his breakfast I packed a few things to eat. We babbled on about seeing rare birds, and ocean freighters far out at sea.

We found a path not far behind the house; our goal was to find a high dune close to the sea for an observation point. We made our way with some difficulty as the dune grass was so thick and in places impenetrable that we continually had to circumnavigate the hillocks, steeper than they had appeared from a distance. We stumbled on tern nests, raised flocks of gulls, and sent rabbits scurrying. Our progress caused a wildlife ruckus that made clear the intention to reclaim the land once we had passed. Behind us we could see the birds settle down again.

Sander carried the tripod and a blanket. I had the telescope slung over my left shoulder and also carried the picnic basket loaded with drinks and food. The telescope had steel parts and thick, old-fashioned lenses, and by the time we reached the highest row of dunes overlooking the sea I was glad to put it down. The tide was out, just turning; the beach here blended into marshland and bird reserve. We found a spot, nestled between two rises protected somewhat from the wind, and set up the tripod as low as possible so that we could sit on the blanket and see through it. I had made up a project for us. We'd brought a pad and pen and would record the names of as many ships from as many lands as possible — we could already see four on the horizon — and later look them up in the island newspaper where their origins, cargoes, tonnage were listed. Sander had first look and right away he shouted, "I can see the name, Ja-la-ka-la — Bombay!"

"You're making it up," I teased and he leaned aside so I could have a look. He was right. The Indian ship jumped into view, with its — to me — romantic-sounding name. We wrote it down, the first on our list, and in just a few minutes we had three names: the other two, closer to shore, Dutch sailing yachts. The fourth boat was barely visible, still too far away to identify, so we went exploring.

There was wildlife everywhere, which surprised me. I had not associated Dutch dunes with animal life. We started searching for as many different kinds of bird feathers as we could find and had brought along a bird book which identified the species by feathers and calls. Sander liked this very much, much the same as collecting shells I suppose. Before long he had twice as many as I, two large handfuls, which I insisted were all from the same bird and he vigorously denied. We took back our treasures and spread them out on the blanket. Not only had he collected more than I but his were also better, more intact, not scruffy ones with parts missing. As far as I could tell there were at least fourteen different birds: gulls and terns, plovers, kites, sand pipers.

He wore an adult's long-sleeved white shirt hanging open outside his Levi cut-offs. They could not have been his before his mother cut the legs for him because they were too big, and as he wore them with no belt they sagged down exposing his underwear. The shirt flapped in the wind; he treated it like a cape, running down a sand hill whooping like an Indian. He was already brown and his eyebrows were bleached glimmering streaks on his tanned face. I took one of the feathers and put it in his hair. He did the same to me, leaning close, his body smelling sweet, not at all of sweat. I ran a feather over his chest and he squirmed. He leaned back on his haunches and I tied a red bandana around his head that I'd had in my back pocket. Perhaps I still retained too much of my American childhood, I thought: Indians and feathers and red headbands.

Eleven is an awkward age. His hands are getting out of proportion to his wrists and his knees are knobby. He has a shrill voice when he shouts, piercing and aggravating. His thighs are smooth, lean and muscular, his shoulders are bony, the flesh taut. Sometimes he keeps his mouth open when he reads or watches television, and his mother tells him this is not well-bred. He makes too much noise when he eats. His forehead appears at first to be higher and broader than the rest of his face, and sometimes delicate worry lines appear there that I want to smooth away. He is careless about his body, or perhaps just not selfconscious about its abilities. He tosses himself here and there, rolls on the ground, does cartwheels and back flips.

He is very vain. He combs his beautiful, thick light brown hair twenty times this way and that before he gets it right, pats it, presses it, curls a lock behind his ear. He knows his eyes are special, hazel-green, flecks of blue and intelligence. A girl at school told him he had beautiful eyes, another girl told him he was beautiful and during swimming class still another said he had a beautiful body. He told me all of this with matter-of-fact pride. Beautiful children know they are beautiful; they are told. His feet are big and he does not like them, perhaps he is afraid that they will embarrass him by betraying an uncertainty. Beautiful: I did not like the word myself. Beauty was dangerous, something you did not wish to dare. You could worship, adore, stand in awe of beauty, but somehow it was never quite accessible. I liked to think he was too grown this way and that out of proportion to be beautiful.

Sander's body was all quivers and restlessness. He liked to be tickled and would tease me until I chased him. Sometimes he would come to where I was sitting and, standing between my legs, would lean towards me and softly call me a jerk or pretend, gently, that he was going to take away the book I was reading. I would put it down and smile and he would lean further, his eyes large, and I would then put my hands upon his waist and gently squeeze. Sometimes too he would blow softly in my face, which aroused me very much, and once, when I did the same to him, he went all still.

Today in the dunes we were wrestling and rolling around and I noticed he had changed his underwear before going out and was no longer wearing the pale blue pair. "You changed your underwear," I exclaimed, it more or less popping out of me in surprise. He pushed his Levis down a bit: white cloth with a red seal design. I laughed — I hoped he knew affectionately — and grabbed him again. He shrieked and I thought he would bring every soul within hearing distance to his rescue. He curled into a ball to avoid my tickling, but when I stopped threw himself on me and tried fiercely to tickle me back, as young animals pounce and roll and kick in a playful frenzy.

"Seals," I said teasing him. "Where did you get those seals..." I was leaning on my elbow looking down at him. I said quietly, trying to imitate a child's chant, "Sander with seals on his underpants..."

I was leaning on my elbow above him. Desire rushed at me and swept me up, a raft without power caught in strong water. I was staring in his eyes, and could feel my face go all red and my body responding. I paused; his hands were at his side and he glanced at me seriously, his eyes wide. I felt breathless, and also afraid. His face was flushed. He stared at something far away. His shirt lay spread open on his bare chest and I could see his breath becoming more labored. I looked down and saw the small metal clasp of the zipper glinting. All this within perhaps a second. Then, he reached down and unsnapped his top button. He closed his eyes. I pushed back the denim cloth fly fold until the entire outline of his erection lay bare. I could measure it now, tautly nestled there amongst the cotton and seals. The wind blew above our heads, warm and fresh. We could hear it from where we lay on the blanket nestled in our shallow dish of sand but not feel it on our hot skin. I said softly, "They're nice seals," and touched just the top of his briefs, my fingertips causing a shiver to run through his stretched frame. I noticed his toes curling. I bent closer. He smelled of sea air and green blended things, of Dutch winds, and his own desire. I ran a fingertip across him and he shuddered, ran my fingers over his stomach wanting him to feel pleasure and pushed them beneath the band. "Sander," I whispered, bending and pressing my face against the side of his, taking him in hand, squeezing gently but firmly. He kept his eyes closed and said nothing, and as gently as I could given my excitement I pressed my lips first against his neck and then began to slide slowly down his body.

August 18th.
Sander has been waxing enthusiastic about our secret place and how many boats and birds we could see through our telescope and has obviously made it seem quite alluring. As we were getting ready to leave the house Marijke said she might join us today with her paints, and asked how she could find it — our male bonding club, our secret garden, our pirate cave. I explained that it was very difficult to find because we did not follow any set path. We headed off east in the direction of the bird reserve towards what we could see as being the highest dune; after about fifteen minutes there was a higher clump of grass than those around and near it a concrete slab remaining from the war, perhaps an anti-tank obstacle or a buried bunker, we could not tell. Straight past there keeping

a glimpse of sea on the left, after about another five minutes were two dunes between which there was a flat space. We ourselves could only retrace our steps with considerable difficulty, having memorized a series of markers: this piece of scrub brush, this wizened pine, and I was afraid that she might get lost. She raised her eyebrows but did not reply.

I wondered if the possibility of her stumbling upon us worried Sander. As we set off he did not say anything about her joining us, but as we got further from the house and the intricacy of the path confused even us and we finally only found the spot with considerable difficulty he said, "No one'll ever find us here."

We set up our small camp site, the telescope on its tripod, and removed our shirts. Sander had first look today and was quiet. I sat next to him, and he leaned a bit against me. I tried to put my arm around his shoulder, but he moved away. I had imagined him stretched sensuously as before on the blanket. I would concentrate all my attention into my fingertips as they grazed the surface of his warm, smooth legs. But he seemed angry today and I moved away a bit, giving him room, letting him be. When we started eating he suddenly threw a sloppy half-eaten plum at me, not entirely as a joke.

"Heh," I said, "don't throw food at me."

"I will if I want," he said in this brattish voice that had often irritated me in the past. Taking the top layer of bread off his tuna sandwich he made as if he was going to throw it at me.

"Don't. Don't do it," I said sternly, but he leaned over and smeared it on my arm and I looked down at it disgustedly. "Christ, why did you do that! What the hell is wrong with you today, you little animal." I took out my handkerchief to wipe away the tuna and mayonnaise. It seemed disgusting to me, and I wondered how I could have ever thought of eating such a mess. He stuck out his tongue and suddenly started growling like a dog and grabbing my other arm he pretended he would bite it. "Don't do it, Sander. Don't bite me." He opened his mouth and put his teeth on it. "Don't do it," I again warned, but slowly he bit me. I had to reach down and pull his mouth away but having succeeded he flung himself at me and tried to push me down to the ground. He was not laughing at all. I tried to push him away but he fought more fiercely and suddenly we were rolling around together, and he was trying to bite me again, first my arm and then my shoulder and then my arm again.

I fended him off. "Stop it. Stop. I don't want you to bite me." He was trying to kick me and his face was screwed up with great intensity. I managed to pin him down. He pursed his lips as if he were going to spit at me, letting the spit form and dribble a little out of his mouth. I tried to tickle him, but the spots where he had been fiendishly ticklish yesterday were not at all ticklish today. He pushed his head against my lower chest, straining against me. His body was overheated from the exertion He was trying to pinch me now and I had to fend this off too. I grabbed his hand and he twisted it this way and that. "I'll let go of it if you stop trying to pinch me." I let go and for a moment he was still, but then suddenly, curled up as he was, he managed to pounce at me again. I was a bit breathless and wanted him to stop. We were not saying anything. I tried to take hold of his hands again but he twisted this way and that. He was almost feverishly hot and as I tried to get some control of him I realized he was now pressing himself against my leg and squirming. I let go of his hands and took the risk of having him bite or kick me again by putting my arms around him. I hugged him, and suddenly he broke away.

We sat together quietly for a while and finished our lunch. He wanted to walk down to the beach, and he ran ahead of me, but when we were on the last dune rise before the sea he sat down waiting, and did not want to go further. I sat next to him. His arms hugged his knees. He let me put my arm around him and I stroked his shoulder and arm.

We could see the beach from where we sat, although here it was more marsh and wetlands and no one walked there. Far out over the water grey clouds were forming and I thought they might cloak the sun in an hour or two. I did not want to leave. He turned his head and studied me in silence with what

I thought was great curiosity, a look I had seen when he mused over his rock collection. He did not sat anything, but he lay back on the sand and taking my hand placed it on himself. I thought afterwards how the warm, bare sand was so natural a home, more a rough nest, welcoming to our naked bodies.

August 20th.
All hell broke loose with Marijke today. What seems to have triggered it was a phone call from Cees saying that after thinking it over he wants to go back to an end of September opening for her show. Of course, they had an argument. If that were not bad enough Niek called her also and, though she will not talk about it, he must have said something about Sander living with him because I heard her say that it was out of the question and it was better for Sander if he were in the city. The entire day she banged around the house in a foul mood, and this evening as I was sitting alone in the kitchen having a cup of tea and reading she came in to get some coffee. It is a very peaceful room, and I enjoy sitting at the table by the wide sliding doors overlooking the garden. Sander was in his room, building a model sailing ship. I had helped him for awhile with the difficult rigging. I could not imagine a more peaceful evening. My sunburnt back was itching, peeling a bit, and when Marijke came in I was awkwardly trying to scratch it.

"Sander is getting too much sun," she said.

He had taken a mild burn on the tops of his legs the first couple of days we had spent in the dunes, but these had already tanned. I did not reply.

She said, "The two of you are spending a lot of time out in the dunes." I glanced up at her. She was standing with her back to the sink, her hands gripping the edge, and was not looking directly at me. I remembered that a couple of days before Sander had been taking a shower and had nonchalantly walked naked the few paces from the bathroom to his bedroom. She had been standing in the hallway, and had made a remark about his tanning evenly all over.

I said nothing and she continued, "I don't know what

the two of you are doing." When I still did not reply she said, though more angrily now, "There are limits you know."

"Of course there are limits. I have a lot of respect for Sander," I said.

"Do you?" she said.

I knew I must be frightened but could hardly feel it, perhaps going a bit into a state of shock. My heart was beating fast. My mind was blank and I honestly could think of nothing to say.

She went on, "Do you honestly think that Sander is old enough to know what he wants? Do you really think that?"

"It seems so to me."

"At eleven." She said it very sarcastically. "You really think so."

"Yes. I care about him."

Her voice rose a notch. "And you think he's old enough to deal with all the adult complications you seem to be willing to foist on him even though you care about him. And I suppose you're also going to tell me that you would never take advantage of him or put him in jeopardy in any way, or coerce him into anything. After we spoke about it already, and I thought we had an understanding."

Her rage was not that far from the surface and I felt threatened. A trickle of cold sweat ran down my side. I thought of the moment in the dunes when he had pushed my hand away and I had stopped. I thought of the moment too when he had pushed himself against me and I had continued. These, I had accepted. I did not know what to say. Anything I said would be so far from Marijke's reality.

I said, "Marijke, you're upset over the gallery and Niek right now and do you really want to talk about this?" I lowered my voice because I did not want Sander to hear. "Sander's a handful. I mean I don't think I idealize him or anything, but I think he understands, knows a lot. About his father, himself; at least as far as I can tell from what he says. He certainly seems to me to know what he does or doesn't want."

"And the consequences as well? I suppose you're going

to tell me that."

Her hands were still gripping the side of the sink. It was extremely difficult for her, I knew that, but also for me. The dunes flashed through my mind; I felt the wind blowing over the surface of our skin; propped on our elbows we were watching a boat out at sea. I must have been very upset, though I felt calm. I said, "I like Sander; I want his friendship. I would try hard not to do anything to risk that."

"How can you say that? How can you stand there and say that?" She turned and poured herself a glass of water, and with her back to me said resentfully, "You're glued to each other all the time. It's not healthy."

"He's upset, about his father, about the break-up between the two of you."

She turned back angrily to me again. "You don't have to tell me about my son. What you're really saying is that he's vulnerable right now and anyone can take advantage of him."

That made me angry now. I did not think I was taking advantage of Sander's need for support. I felt like telling her what Sander had said about his father trying to blackmail him emotionally into joining him, and thank God I checked myself, kept Sander's confidence.

I said quietly, "I try to be responsible with him," but it sounded trite and stupid.

"Responsible. So you're willing to tell me nothing is going on. I dare you to look straight at me and tell me that you and he, out there in the dunes..." She stopped herself, and then, crossing to the table, continued, "Sander is too young for all of this. I don't care what you say. He's just too young for all of this. I don't want him hurt. Not now with everything else up in the air." She put the glass down on the table too abruptly, and it banged, spilling water. I could see her hand was shaking; she fumbled for a cigarette.

She said, "It might be better if you just left him alone. Left us both alone. Just left." She sat down at the table and lit her cigarette, shaking the match too vigorously.

My anger came to the surface. Everything was at risk. I did not say anything immediately. I looked out the window.

I wanted to say that I was just going along moment to moment with Sander, trying to be present for him. I wanted to say that I found it difficult; that I felt as if he were judging me all the time, not on any conscious level, but judging me nevertheless; as if he were demanding perfect attention from me and God forbid I were to fail. I felt at the edge. I am not sure what made me think it at this moment, but I thought that if I went on now with the conversation this would extend my responsibility to her. If I wanted to fight for my involvement with Sander, and I knew at that moment overwhelmingly that I did, it also meant accepting Marijke and all that entailed.

I turned angrily from the window and broke our silence. I said fiercely, "No, I can't accept that; leaving. I can't accept that. What are you going to do, punish him now, isolate him, give him the impression that something dirty and awful has happened? And what about you? We've been friends."

"Friends! And when my back is turned, when I'm off with Cees or painting, you've been... Don't even dare talk to me about friends."

I wanted to bang chairs and break something, and knew she must have felt the same way, so I stopped suddenly, but then added more calmly, "I'm not willing to just walk out of here and let Sander be burdened with guilt."

"It's not your choice. It's mine. Sander is not your responsibility. He's mine."

I had thought all along that Sander was in his bedroom but suddenly, as if we both sensed it together, Marijke and I turned and Sander was standing in the kitchen doorway. He was extremely pale and I could see he was shaking.

"Sander," Marijke said, and her one word was enough to trip his response. He shouted, "I'm not going to live with him! I'm not!" Marijke said calmly, "Sander, that's not what we were talking about."

"I know what you were talking about. I heard you talking. I'm not a baby. I heard you." He suddenly picked up a glass off the counter near where he was standing and flung it against the wall, smashing it into ten thousand pieces. He rushed over to the table and hurled things to the ground, overturning a chair. There was a moment of complete confusion and I do not know how the next moment came about, but Marijke and I must have reacted in the same way because suddenly we were holding on to Sander and trying to prevent him from harming himself. He was shouting and crying, "Stop it. Stop it. I don't want you to fight. I don't want to live with him. I won't." We could hardly hold him. He kicked at us and thrashed. Marijke started to cry and it was all a mess for quite some time before we all calmed down.

There is no ending to this. I made a pot of tea. Hot tea with milk and lots of honey was good for shock, someone had told me. The three of us sat in the kitchen for hours it seemed and talked, and that was, perhaps, being Dutch. The conversation went around the table, and around, and around, and nothing really was settled, nor entirely ended either.

As I sit here writing this now they are both in bed and the house is very quiet, and I do not know what to think. It is now nearly one. I have the window open a crack though it is a bit cold. The air is heavy and smells of rain. I wonder if my life will ever be the same again.

Part Three: Friesland

1. Thursday Afternoon, March 1st

Sander has gotten over being angry with Michiel for the incident on the tram a few days ago. I had to coax the story out of him, but it seems as if Michiel apologized in a roundabout way. When Sander is angry he ignores you, as if to say, "Go to hell; I don't need you." Having been the brunt of this I know how manipulative it can be. He was ignoring Michiel, and Michiel blurted out — at least as Sander told it with pleasure, "The next time that creep insults your father I'll punch him out."

He wanted me to go over this afternoon. The two of them have to make a video film for school and they were having trouble coming up with a theme. I was still feeling a bit under the weather and wasn't sure I was in the most creative of moods, but anything short of hospitalization was not going to impress him very much. I could have said, 'not going to impress the stoical Dutch very much', as less than a 102-degree fever never justifies absence from work, school, or, in this case, helping Sander. He coaxed and cajoled and I said, "Put your mother on," but she was at the gallery and I called her there.

She was in a bad mood. Niek had wandered in acting conspiratorial about something having to do with me; it was the last thing she had wanted to deal with. I told her that Niek and I had an appointment for Saturday before the party, and no doubt it would turn out to be nothing. "Not this time," she said, but when I asked her what she meant she said dismissively, "Oh, nothing; nothing." She did not have anything specific in mind, and added that he said he wanted me to phone him. It annoyed me. I could imagine his overly dramatized tone, "Have Will phone me right away!" I had been in all day, so what kind of a game was he playing? I was not going to get into it; she sounded tired and I changed the subject to Sander. Whenever Michiel was over they created a mess. She might be getting back home late as she had to give a talk at some women's group. The neighbor was going to baby-sit, she said wearily, but she supposed she could call her and I could go instead. There was food in the refrigerator; all I had to do was heat it. I called Sander back and said I would be there in about an hour.

As I walked over to their house I felt a bit shaky, and even broke into a sweat. I rang the bell — no one answered. It was windy and cold, and I did not much appreciate being kept outside. I tried the door and it was open. I called out from the bottom of the stairs. No one. The stereo had been left on — I turned it off; the patio door was ajar, and I closed it. Wherever they had gone he should not have left the house unlocked.

I went upstairs to his room. No note; the video camera discarded on the bed amongst a detritus of candy and gum wrappers, school books, clothing and comic books. I pushed things aside and sat down. Sander's room: the requisite garish rock-star posters, the strewn parts of Lego models, the sport socks fuming from the corner, the computer games, a water pistol sticking out from under the corner of the dresser, kicked by a careless foot. Sometimes he would not open the window for days and the room became, as now, stale with boy smells, discarded food — sweaty and pungent things. Marijke rushed in now and then in a frenzy and things were aired, removed and washed, only for the accretion to begin again, as visual as some time-lapse film showing the growth of a tangled forest floor. Perhaps it is all a phase with which one needs to be patient, of discovering himself, his body, his gender. When he blasts his music I cannot go anywhere near there, the sound perimeters become for me a kind of castle wall I do not want to besiege.

Not everything is conformist, his own personality glints here and there through the various veneers: plants in pots on the window sill that he has grown from seed; the watercolor portrait of him by Marijke in a wooden frame he himself chose, a nude photograph of him taken by Niek several years ago. On his desk, his computer and computer games, stacks of school books and novels, but also the favorite shells and rocks from his collection, spilled over onto a cherry-wood shelf with fluted edge he built in his grandfather's workshop. He has painted his room pale yellow and picked for the window plain white, vitrage curtains and a dark green shade, now half pulled down. On his dresser there is a snapshot in a brass filigree frame of the three of them, taken three or four years ago. They looked happy together then. It is not the room of a street waif. It reflects a certain sophistication, bourgeois privileges.

I very early learned what his room signified to him — a refuge where he could go to sulk when he was being nagged to death and browbeaten with demands. At first he resented my entering so private a world. He would frown a little when I knocked on the door and tried to draw him out of his mood. Before the separation it was his father's unreasonable haranguing him about some small detail that made him feel so misused: not flushing the toilet, not picking up his dirty clothes, leaving his bike blocking the entrance; but afterwards it was his mother's endless droning on about his lack of concern for her, his failure to do his chores at the right time, his not having showered, that sent her into a rant and him pouting up the stairs. It took him a long time to get over the feeling that somehow when he'd locked himself away in his room I was part of that outside world too that he was shutting out, and I too should not be let in.

Why should I accept that? For his sake I tried to divert attention from himself. When the three of us had been in the car together I would sit in the back seat with him and play road games — I spy, and license plates — keeping him out of their hair. On one occasion, as we were riding home late from one of Niek's openings, I made up a very long and involved story that went on and on until he fell asleep, curled up against me, a car blanket over us — a hundred things one could do, so small it was hard to assign much importance to them.

Sander's room had become for me some place alive, erotic and close to nature. I would sometimes stretch out on his bed and imagine him as a somehow still warmly pervasive spirit lingering in the sheets, blankets, pillows, fiber, and fabric.

I went downstairs and made myself some tea. Perhaps I should phone Niek while I was waiting? Tempted to play the game? He would not have arrived back at the farm yet. The alcohol sometimes made him seem menacing to me, almost sinister, as that evening at the farm, when I was sitting on Sander's bed looking at his shells with him, and Niek appeared in the doorway. That must have been October, after the summer on Texel...

2. October, November, December, Last Year

October 10th.
Since Niek and Marijke's separation has become somewhat official I have been visiting Niek at the farm: three or four weekends since the end of August, sometimes with Sander, sometimes alone. Niek has had several people visiting for the day that he has wanted me to meet; there always seems to be an excuse. Last weekend it was a museum curator from Frankfurt.

Sander went with me. He has some new shells for his collection that his uncle Theo, Niek's older brother, brought back for him from the west coast of Florida. He is an eccentric, and something of a hero to both Sander and Niek. He made a lot of money in the stock exchange and drifts around the world on his schooner doing what he likes. He keeps the boat in the Dutch Caribbean and spends most of his time there, returning here for occasional business forays. He promised that Sander could spend a summer on his boat, but keeps making excuses, so it has never happened, although Sander does not seem to hold it against him. Over dinner Sander waxes on and on about the shells: they are very special; they would cost a lot of money if he had to buy them here; no one brings him shells as nice as his uncle Theo does. He is eager to show them off to me and rushes through his meal. I can see that Niek is increasingly put out with him, perhaps out of sibling jealousy with Theo as much as anything that Sander is doing. He gets angry — makes an abusive remark in front of the curator and his wife; Sander is embarrassed, angry; he sulks, asks to be excused, and goes up to his room.

Niek's mood becomes unpleasantly tense. I am afraid it will be an excuse for him to drink a lot, and am both right and wrong. He gets increasingly drunk, and mean, but anything could have precipitated the drinking. Niek, the curator and I go into the living room to digest, and talk about photography. Loo is not here this week and the curator's wife dutifully accepts the task of making the coffee and serving it to us on a tray. I feel uncomfortable. It is not even her house and yet Niek somehow manages to impinge rigid gender roles on his surroundings, something that Marijke bitterly resented. The curator's wife is very gracious and accepts the task with humor while the men retire to smoke their cigars and have their brandy! It might have been a Victorian manor house in England. I have to say that Niek looked thin and strained. He eases his slightly tipsy fragile frame into the armchair opposite me and immediately pours himself another large whiskey.

I have not been at the gallery for more than a week and want to catch up with the news. The new exhibition, photogravures by a 1920s Dutch photographer, Richard Polak is doing extremely well. They are imitations of Dutch master paintings, but very well done and amazingly we have sold five already, though the prices are quite low. The curator had seen them today and suddenly announces that he wants to buy some and on the spot reserves three. We have to send details and an invoice. The mood becomes more upbeat. Niek makes a cynical joke that perhaps the tide is turning for photography in the Netherlands? Somehow I do not believe it.

Music drifts through the hallways from Sander's room, the ever increasing sound of an approaching train. I get up and close the hall door, but we still find ourselves talking louder, and still louder, to compensate. He must know it will make Niek angry, and he must be baiting him. Niek twists in his chair, a fierce expression on his face. I say that I had promised to go see his new shells and had better do it now before he blasts us out of house and home.

But I do not go immediately. The curator wants my opinion about the current photo auction season in New York. How do I think the recession will affect sales? Can I predict any trends? Niek brings up a gallery problem. We have exclusive rights to sell all the work of a certain Dutch photographer who has now sold some prints to a San Francisco dealer without consulting us or paying us our commission. He claims he did not think he had to. Perhaps the photographer is being a bit shrewd, but I suggest we simply remind him of the terms of the contract, that is, assume he will act honorably. Niek says that he thinks we should forget our commission because if we demand it the photographer will harbor resentments. The curator laughingly agrees. We go back and forth on it for several minutes before deciding we should make it clear to the man that we think we should receive our commission, but we should not insist on it either. It is half an hour before I can go upstairs to join Sander.

He has spread the new shells out on the bed and is labelling them with their scientific names when I walk in. Several books are open around him and he is looking up the scientific name of each new one before arranging it carefully in a wooden box lined with blue cloth. He writes their names in ink on small squares of white paper he cuts himself carefully with a scissors. He tells me why each is special. This reddish-hued one is a conch, he says. "It's a marine gastropod," he adds without looking in the book. The horny plate at the end of the shell he points out is a claw. He makes it interesting to me. We are sitting very close to one another on the bed and he leans against me trustingly, his head lowered. His hands are fid-geting nervously, his long fingers reaching first for this shell, then for that, turning it, holding it up to the light. His fine brown hair, the side of his smooth neck, his fresh energy draw me into his sphere. I feel an urge to taste the salt of his skin. He looks up at me. I cannot read his expression.

And then Niek suddenly appeared at the door of Sander's room. Sander's music was still on, but he had lowered it, though it was loud enough for us not to have heard him approaching. I look up and he is standing there in the doorway, whiskey glass in hand. It gave me quite a start. I had my arm around Sander's shoulder and we were huddled together, but both of us pulled apart at the same time.

Niek said, "There's apricot flan for dessert; you didn't have any." It sounded bizarre. Sander scooped his shells into a pile but did not answer.

October 16th.
Marijke and Sander are arguing a lot; a tense atmosphere in the Oude Waal house, both of their nerves frayed. A few days ago I made an innocent mistake which I hope goes no further. Sander has been coming by after school for the past couple of weeks. He asked me yesterday if he could stay over this weekend, probably just to get away from some of the turmoil, and, of course, I said he had to telephone and first ask his mother's permission. I could hear her say through the phone, even from a distance, "No, absolutely not! I want you home by five." In the background things were being banged around: a pot, a cupboard door. Sander started to pout. "She says no. Now she's mad at me again."

"I don't think she's mad at you. Besides, you can stay over another time, maybe next weekend. She's been upset lately. It's just hard for her right now, and you too I suppose."

Sander said, "We fight all the time. I'd rather live with you."

I wanted to embrace him, instantly help him pack his bags, but I said cooly, "What would Niek say?"

"He doesn't care about me either. He has Loo and anyway he cares more about his drinking that about me."

I was not sure what to say and pondered it for a moment or two. What I thought he meant was not that he really wanted to come and live with me but that he needed to know that somewhere he could find some security. It was peaceful and quiet in my apartment, and I gave him my undivided attention.

I finally gave him a hug and said, "You can always count on me. I won't let you down." His mood brightened.

October 21st.
An odd conversation in the car last night as Niek, Loo, Sander and I were driving back from the opening of a new museum in Cologne...

We had received an invitation from the curator of the Photography Division. When we arrived there were television cameras and celebrities everywhere: the mayor, Minister of Culture, the Dutch ambassador, famous photographers. We were dressed very casually in Levis; Niek was wearing a sweater with holes in it and I a rather ragged jacket, having come straight from matting and hanging a new show without changing. There were hundreds of people milling about and we thought we only had to make our faces known and leave, but no sooner were we there than a television crew came up to us. It turns out that we were listed as the official Dutch delegation and they wanted to film us for the evening news. Niek speaks fluent German and did a very noble job of it. Loo, Sander and I kept well to the side.

It was nearly midnight before we began the three-hour drive back to Amsterdam. Loo was feeling nauseous and had stretched out on the back seat with a blanket over her. Sander was squeezed between Niek and me in the front of their Citroen, and no sooner were we on the road than he and Loo both fell asleep.

I said something to Niek about helping to keep him awake. Thank God he had not been drinking much. He replied a bit caustically that he never fell asleep while driving. He drove very fast, much too fast for my liking. He crouched over the wheel, gripping it tightly in his hands, as if coaxing even more speed from it, or identifying with the danger, perhaps. His fierce concentration brought out lines on his taut forehead. The well-tuned car hardly made a sound, but I watched the trees speed by with ever increasing velocity, and ever increasing trepidation. Did he really have that much control of the machine?

Niek was jumping distractedly from this to that subject. Sander woke up, sat up in a daze, rubbed his eyes, took his shoes off and curled up cat-like, staking my lap as his territory. I rubbed his back, and glanced out at trees, houses, lights in a blur as we sped past. Niek fiddled with the radio but shut it off. He has given up smoking on his doctor's advice because of his lungs, but eats chocolate instead. He took a bar out of the glove compartment and offered me some. The highway, though it was a Saturday, was nearly deserted: an occasional truck, a lone car, which we sped by in quick gasps. I did not dare to look at the speedometer. His broken string of disconnections gave me no idea of what he wanted to say: "The gallery's doing fine; Sander seems happy in his new Montessori school; have to show you my new series of photos, I'm pleased with them. The opening was boring. The curator's a nice guy. Buys my work. You have to suck up to him a bit. He's good for a few sales. German collectors are xenophobic..." When I tried to intrude a comment, instead of continuing the line of talk, he jumped to something else instead. He seemed to tire of this after a few minutes and a bit of silence.

I said that I could not sleep in cars. Even when I was a child I couldn't. My mother use to say to me, when we were going on vacation, that I should take a nap, that it would make the time go by faster, but I'd sit with my face glued to the window so I wouldn't miss anything. "I envy those two," I added.

Niek replied, "Sounds like you. We were poor. Never travelled much when I was a child. Never saw much more than Rotterdam. My father was a socialist and said a car was evil, but what he meant was that he couldn't afford it. Did you get in to see Jerzy's show tonight at the museum? It reminded me a little of our house when I was a kid. Peeling walls, kids with no shoes. Of course he fakes it, for effect, to make it look like nineteenth-century London or Warsaw, Dickens or wherever it is in his imagination."

I had seen the Szymanowski exhibition and had liked it quite a lot. His work was very popular right now, although, no doubt, it had been something of a political move to feature an East European photographer in the opening of a German museum. His works were theatrical, flamboyant color prints deliberately staged to make them reflect various eighteenth or nineteenth-century icons: nude girls on Boucher divans, or a nude woman stepping into a Degas bath. There were references to circus or Folies Bergères paintings and posters. The backgrounds were self-consciously decadent, though I was not sure I agreed with Niek that their purpose was to suggest poverty so much as to imitate the atmosphere of nineteenth-century erotica. He played with gender in a modern way, a boy erotically uncovering a nipple, a nude girl with short hair made up to look like a boy. I knew that Niek was acquainted with him, that they had met at the photo festival in Arles a few years before, and that Niek had made a few portraits of him. Jerzy also had a home in the south of France and Niek, Marijke and Sander had stayed there for several days.

"I have all his books and have seen several of his one-man shows. I've been interested in his work for several years," I said. "Sometimes it's a bit too forced, too deliberate and selfconscious, but at its best it's quite daring, beautifully balanced, wry. I've heard that there's a new book coming out soon."

"I saw the new work at his house last year. I think it's his best. More imitation nineteenth-century. You probably would like it. It's very well composed. Intellectual East European, a French influence. He's dating the photographs 1890s, like '15th October, 1892'. You know, I'm not surprised you like his work. You should get to meet him. Maybe the next time I go to visit you can come too."

Sometimes I preferred hard-edged documentary black and white work to staged photography, which could sometimes be so pretentious. I felt that as soon as a photograph was staged an idea was imposed upon it and that photographs might better represent found things, even found ideas, perfectly caught, such as Cartier-Bresson did, but that was not some sort of law.

"I think that what one has to say is that what Jerzy does he does better than anyone. You know him a little don't you? What's he like?"

"You should visit him, see his studio, especially the house in France. He's very friendly. Lives quite simply. Especially in his apartment in Warsaw. Nothing much. No microwave. I didn't even see a television. He does like music. He's warm, kind, generous. Lots of people around. Of course, there are all those photographs of little girls. Boys too, but the girls are more the obsession. Being around his studio even a few days I can see why they might be. They're beautiful. Affectionate. Very attractive. I have enough of it inside me, I think, to understand just how attractive, but I would never do anything about it. I suppose it's in all of us. We're all a little paedophile."

"Oh I don't know," I said, I think quite sincerely. "I've heard people say that but I don't really think it's true. I mean as humans we can all imagine almost anything and feel almost any impulse but being able to imagine something doesn't make someone into something. It's more than that — what makes our desire what it is and turns it into an identity."

"What is it then?"

"Oh God, I don't know. Perhaps..." I realized selfconsciously that all that time I had had my hand on Sander's hair. Niek was glancing back and forth between me and his driving. I supposed that, in his oblique way, he was fishing for a confidence I was not willing to give under those circumstances. All I could think of to say was that being what we are means that our situations are total, that the desire was not some adjunct piece stuck on but an element in a totality. If it was not of a whole then I didn't see how it could be real. Desire was a reality.

I added, "I suppose it has something to do with the diversity of creation, and freedom..." But I was afraid that I was beginning to sound pompous or grandiose and shut up.

Niek said, "I don't think I really know what you mean."

"Well, it's the best I can do for the moment."

I thought that this was the last of it, but after a moment's hesitation he reiterated, "Well, I would never do anything about it."

November 5th.
Sander phoned me on Thursday to ask me if I would take him up to his father's farm for the weekend. Yes, he had already asked his mother; no, she could not go with us because she had to work, and, yes, it was all right with his father. Monday was a school holiday and the plan was that we would both stay over until late Monday evening. The farm is in the middle of nowhere and, as Niek usually spends a lot of time in the darkroom, I could easily bring my own work with me. Sander has a way of leaving out 'little things' that have in the past created big misunderstandings, so I asked him to put his mother on. She had spoken to Niek herself and he had said that he wanted to talk to me about something, but had not said what. She was sure he genuinely wanted us both there. I was certainly welcome to use her car.

When I arrived Friday morning to fetch him, Sander must have been waiting behind the door; he flung it open instantly, swinging his knapsack and ready to leave. "Keep your britches on," I said, not sure he understood the American slang. He screwed up his face at me. I told him to calm down and at least let me get the car keys. He dangled them in front of me. I shouted up the stairs for Marijke and she said something about the car being two doors down. As we were ready to drive away she came outside. I rolled down the window. Sander was already playing with the radio dials and shuffling through the tapes. She went through the usual maternal list: homework, toothbrush, change of clothes? Sander's answer was to blare the music. She became exaggeratedly angry. I reached over and turned it off.

"Any idea why Niek wants to see me?" I asked.

"No. He doesn't tell me anything anymore. Probably some gallery thing."

Sander impatiently turned the music up but as swiftly turned it down again. He removed the rap tape that he had been blasting at us and put in Mozart.

I said through the window to Marijke, "I think this creature next to me is trying to tell me something."

"He's been awful lately." She bent a little farther down to see Sander: "Don't get in your father's way, and don't tease the farmer next door."

"I won't."

"The last time he was there the old man next door had to chase him out of his barn and he's still complaining about it to Niek."

"I didn't hear that story."

"I wasn't doing anything!"

"Just remember what I said. I don't want to hear any stories." She straightened and said to me, "When he's in the country he's like an animal. Forgets every manner he's ever learned."

I said, "We'll have to find some hard work for him to keep him out of trouble, like cleaning out the garage or something."

Sander took the Mozart tape out and put the rap one back in; closing his eyes, pursing his lips, and beating on the dashboard for a drum. Marijke backed away from the car with an expression and gesture that seemed to mean, "Good luck with him and better you than me."

At ten-thirty on a Friday morning only a few cars sped along the highway north to Lelystad-Emmelord. A bridge connected the northern polder to the northeastern provinces, the shortest route to the farm. The Dutch landscape was not monotonous to me, perhaps because of having to study it for my book or perhaps because the changing affinities of sky and earth were something I thought no one could find boring: it was a kind of theatrics of clouds and light, sometimes a dramatic clash, sometimes a marriage clothed in color. Theories abounded, of course: that the Dutch landscape was a constant confrontation with creationist theology, all wind, water, and light, the stuff of biblical thoughts. Across expanses of meadows crisscrossed by dikes, cows and sheep grazing, the tip of a church spire, the tops of thatched houses caught glints of sun. The air smelled of dung and fresh earth. In the distance a long row of poplars indicated a farm road on which I caught a glimpse of a small, black car moving more slowly than we.

What was I to do with Sander? He was taking everything out of the glove compartment, slinking his way over the front seat into the back and up front again, blaring the radio; he pulled the full ashtray out too quickly and it came away in his hand spilling cigarette butts and ashes all over the floor. I told him sharply to calm down. I managed to get him to talk about his school work. He had a special project to do for the long weekend, write it up, with drawings even. He thought he would make an Indian teepee if I would help him. I had given him the previous Christmas a book about the daily life of a nineteenth-century Dakota Sioux Indian boy and when we had read it together he'd had a hundred questions to ask.

Sander and a Sioux boy, they could not be further apart. The Sioux had a horse, perhaps a blanket, a quiver with arrows, and according to the story at least roamed free. He did not bear the burden of centuries-old culture, the constriction of the closeness of Dutch life and ways; he seemed to be in a way more closely identified with the things and ways of childhood: the spirits in the rocks, wind and birds that Sander dreamed about but did not really worship. For Sander the Dakota boy's world was surrounded by space and silence, a kind of buffer zone where he could do as he pleased without a watchful eye, making up right and wrong as he went along, out of the practicalities and demands of survival.

An image flashed through my mind — Sander in the process of becoming an American Indian: sandy-colored hair, green eyes, classical nose and painted face. He still had some of the dune tan from last summer and the thought of undressing him, of shedding him of his Levi conformity, the black tee-shirt, the prerequisite running shoes and the brand-name underwear in order to build some new cultural identity out of his nudity was a very sympathetic thought to me. I would find a bolt of cloth from which a breech cloth could be fashioned, and adjust it to hang correctly between his sturdy, smooth legs, and perhaps also paint his chest with white streaks until the creature that stood before me, neither Dutch nor quite Indian, was closer in raw life to the boy lying beside me the summer before in the sand.

A teepee was a good idea, I said. The farm had some dwarf apple trees that Niek carefully pruned and some high hawthorn hedges, but nothing much larger than that from which to extract the long sturdy poles necessary, but we could improvise.

We were over the bridge by now north of Lelystad with perhaps only a half hour more to go. I handed Sander the map but he knew the road well and told me to turn off here, turn right there. As we grew closer Sander seemed to grow more pensive, not more nervous the way people become just before they arrive in a place where there are expectations. He slumped into pensiveness, staring vacantly out of the window. I glanced at him.

He suddenly asked, "What's it like in San Francisco?"

I tried to describe how different it was from Amsterdam, all hills and high buildings, although there were similarities too, good public transportation and trams, but he said that what he meant was what was my apartment like. It was in a new building, I explained, on the crest of a hill not too close to the downtown or the University, but close to shops, schools and a quiet park. I had purchased my apartment with some inheritance money. There was an outdoor swimming pool. I lived on the twelfth floor. From the balcony I could see half the city. I imagined Sander standing there next to me.

"Who's in it now?"

"A teacher and his wife."

"How many bedrooms are there?"

"Two, one is my study."

"Do you have a television?"

"Of course; cable television."

He fell silent. I glanced sideways at him but he was staring ahead at the road. He was sulking a bit, and played with the glove compartment, opening and closing it, and rifling through the contents. I wasn't sure what I should say.

His mind raced on. He exclaimed, "I've got it!"

"What?"

"How we can make the teepee. That canvas in the barn? The one covering the motorbike? We can put a rope between the apple trees and then we can put the tarpaulin over it. Simple, eh?"

That was not exactly a teepee, more a lean-to, I said, but I agreed that it would work just fine. We were on a little side, dike road raised above the terrain. A hundred yards or so along a branch turn sloped downwards towards a few old houses nestled among copses of windswept beech. Niek's was the last one: Friesian red brick with wood trim and gables painted deep Dutch green; separated from the road by the prerequisite ditch and little wooden bridge. The property was long and narrow, about four acres reaching far back to a grove of trees Niek had planted years ago when they had first purchased the farm. I smelled a wood fire as we stepped out of the car. Niek had bought a large, gangling stupid mutt of a dog that came barking and bounding at us, his shaggy fur covered with mud, excitedly leaping at and around us, as we fended him off.

November 12th.
Niek has been browbeating Sander constantly for the last two days; nothing he does is right. At meals he is criticized for his table manners, shouted at for showing reluctance to help with the dishes, told he is a total infant who cannot even keep his feet from smelling. All of this is exaggerated, and quite aggravating to Sander. After all, most of the things for which he is being reprimanded are normal for his age, especially for him.

Niek alternates this with affection. Sander said last night that his shoulder was hurting from lifting the heavy canvas over the clothes line while we were constructing the teepee. Niek had him take his shirt off, put on some ointment, and massaged it in thoroughly. It is confusing. I tried a couple of times gently to intervene but Niek chooses not to hear my admonitions: "Oh, he's just acting his age." Or, "Typical eleven-year-old." When in the darkroom Sander by accident dropped some chemicals on one of Niek's prints, quite destroying it, I said, "He's at a clumsy age. Didn't mean anything by it, I'm sure". But Niek still shouted at him.

He has not exactly left me alone either. There are these games he is playing about the gallery. On the one hand he tells me that I have become the central person there and that he has a good mind to turn it over lock, stock and barrel to me. On the other hand, when I ask him for some of the names and addresses of the French contacts he promised me he is evasive and finds excuses not to give them to me. Has it all to do with ego — or drink? He was supposed to talk to me about something but when I ask him directly what it was he becomes evasive. I rarely see him without a glass or bottle somewhere close by: on the kitchen cupboard a tumbler half filled with whiskey, on the darkroom table a partial bottle of gin. At ten in the morning he asks if I want a glass of wine or a beer!

Late this afternoon I had finally had enough of it and went out for a walk by myself. It was cloudy, cold and windy up on the dike road, but the sharpness was a great relief after the claustrophobic tensions. I walked for a couple of hours and tried not to dwell on Sander, about whom I am beginning to obsess. Sander this, and Sander that — ever Sander.

I dwelt on my book and the Dutch landscape. I do not know why so many people, including the Dutch, dismiss it out of hand as flat and uninteresting. I found a bench along the roadside by a marker describing the history of the dike works and stayed for a while. In all directions I could not see any high-tension wires or billboards, or roads even, except for the one I was on. No planes flew overhead; silent fields around and from where I stood, myself at the center. There is not much photography that even comes close to seventeenth-century painting. The painters were able to filter their effects and remove or shift extraneous details. Photographers have to take the scene as they find it, and found nature is always a bit messy and unkempt (like Sander, Niek would say), which makes it harder for a photograph to communicate the theology of natural perfection and the goodness of creation that was central to the Golden Age painters. But I had already put these thoughts in my book, and wended my way back to the farm.

When I returned I went searching for Sander, but he was not in the teepee or in his clubhouse in the barn, nor in his bedroom or anywhere that I could see. Niek's red darkroom light was on and he'd said he wanted to work uninterruptedly and possibly not even be disturbed for dinner. I went back to Sander's room one last time to check. It was on the ground floor, at the back of the house. There was a glass door in the room that should have led out onto a patio, but the stone tiles had never been laid. The ground there was often muddy and the door rarely used. It stood ajar now, but I could not see any footprints in the soft earth. I stood in his room looking out into the yard, thought I heard a creak and turned to listen. Nothing. And then a sneeze. Sander was lying huddled on the floor in a corner by his bed, curled up inside his sleeping-bag, which I had thought was empty. I sat down on the floor next to him and tried to pull the cloth back, but he was gripping it firmly with his hand and resisted me.

"Sander," I said. "What's the matter? Have you been in here all this time? I've been looking everywhere for you. I thought we were going to finish the teepee. Come on. Let go. It's all right. Come on out of there now." I was pulling gently at the cloth and he finally allowed me to expose his head. His forehead was all sweaty and his face flushed. I smoothed back his hair. "You look sick. Are you all right?"

He would not look at me. "You're upset, aren't you?"

He mumbled something, and tried to pull the cover over his head again. "Come on, now." I said. "You don't have to stay in there. It's all right."

I finally managed to get him up, but could not get much out of him in the way of an explanation. I pieced together a few things: that, while I was out walking, Niek had hollered at him and said that he was always in the way, and that I had promised I would help him this afternoon finish the teepee and maybe go for a walk together and instead I had gone by myself without even asking him. I could think of nothing to say. I put my arms around him and hugged him. His body was almost feverishly hot, but he did not draw back from me.

November 12th. Later.
This evening I went outside again to get some air. I had left Niek, quite drunk, mumbling to himself on the living-room sofa. Sander had retreated hours earlier to his room. I regretted having come. Sander was in a terrible mood, and Niek was impossible. I had not been able to do any work, and the weekend, thank God, was nearly over.

It was about eleven and as I walked around to the back of the house I could see that Sander's light was still on. There was no drape over the glass door; the backyard here faced only fields and trees. I walked up closer, to watch him. He was walking around, doing the ordinary things one does when one is alone. I was a bit embarrassed with myself, but I had never had the opportunity before to observe Sander without his knowing it. He seemed to have gotten over his bad mood already. He was playing with his Lego, building a spaceship. He flew it around the room in his stockinged feet. He threw it in a corner and jumped onto his bed landing on his back and bouncing a couple of times until he could catapult himself to his feet. He did a headstand, letting his feet curve around to touch the wall. There was a chinning bar across his closet doorway and he pulled himself rapidly up and down a few times.

He went to his mirror and rifled around on the top of his dresser until he found a feather, which he tried to stick upright in his hair. It wouldn't stay and he found a red bandana I had given him months before and twisting it into a narrow band tied it around his forehead. He pulled off his shirt and put the white gull feather into the red band. He rifled around in a drawer and found some crayons and described two streaks, one red and one yellow, down either cheek and a black one down his nose. He turned his head this way and that, but not content with that began to paint rings around his upper arms, then made a muscle. A few bright red lines on his chest were added; he clenched his fists and thrust out his chest. He rummaged around in a drawer again, throwing things out of it this way and that, and then the same in a wardrobe, and finally under the bed. He dragged out an old pair of black gym shorts and taking out his Swiss army knife he cut the shorts down the side and cut loose the crotch. He peeled off all his clothes and slipped on the cut shorts. He turned this way and that and cut more cloth from them, painted stripes on his legs in green and brown this time, took the mirror down from atop the dresser and placed it on the floor so he could see himself full length. What was his name now? Who was he? My heart was pounding and I was ready to turn away from the glass when he must have seen my movement. He came to the door. I was very embarrassed and just stood stock still, not smiling, not even lifting a hand to greet him. The patio door was still slightly ajar, and he slid it open. He looked angry, fierce with all this warpaint on. He put a finger to his lip.

I more or less hopped into his room over the spot of soft ground. He was standing opposite me, leaning back against his dresser. I stood awkwardly, silent, but not wanting to be intimidated by an eleven-year-old boy I looked him directly in the eye. He went to his door, listened for a minute, and then locked it. He was still looking at me, still with the same angry furrowed brow and pursed, determined lips. He had not said a word to me, nor I to him. He was leaning against the wall by the door and reaching up behind him switched off the light, then walked over to his bed and stretched himself out. My eyes adjusted. There was enough light to see. I walked over and stood there looking down at him. His arms were resting by his side; he was staring at the ceiling.

I felt confused. Was he offering himself as some kind of sacrifice to me, or as a privilege, a favor given? He seemed entirely in command. His erection had partly pushed aside the nylon cloth. I sat down carefully on the edge of the bed and taking the cloth carefully with two fingers I delicately folded it back to expose him. I placed my left hand over his right side, lowered my head and pressed my lips against the base of his stomach, moved lower, and tenderly, firmly slid him between my lips, feeling the hard, warm sponginess yield to my pressure, his light salt taste rush to my head, maddened again by its utter silken smoothness. I could hardly breathe; it was not hard to hold all his small length in my mouth, savoring and coaxing him to pleasure. He groaned and with his left hand pushed my head down and thrust himself up. His back arched, his legs stretched their full length. He came almost instantly onto my tongue as I moved it side to side to intensify the moment.

I removed my clothes and stretched myself beside him. His eyes were closed tightly. I put my arm around him and coaxed him to turn so that I could hold him in my arms. I pressed my lips against his cheek. It was gradually colder in the room and we slipped beneath the covers. I held him, caressed his back; he shivered a bit. It was very quiet in his room and in the countryside around. Neither of us could fall asleep. He propped himself up on his elbow and now looked down at me.

He said, "If I go back to San Francisco with you, maybe we can live on an Indian reservation."

"Those are in Arizona and Nevada."

"So? We can go there can't we?"

I drew with my fingertips small circles on his shoulders and chest, feeling the texture of filament boy hair along his arms.

"The way you look right now you'd fit right in."

"You like it, don't you?"

I nodded.

"So, can we go then?"

I wanted to say that we could go anywhere, be anywhere. My fingertips descended in slow circles, my other hand lightly raised and brushed along his hair. He was erect again. I thought he would lapse back into silence but he did not. "I wouldn't have to put up with him any more," he said. "I could get a job and make my own pocket money. Have as many GameBoys as I want. You'll see. If you ask them they won't even care. They'll say, sure he can go with you. Good riddance."

We talked for a long while.

December 2nd.
Today, at my apartment, we were rolling around on the living-room floor, wrestling and tickling each other, and making, I might say, such loud shrill shrieking sounds that I am sure we disturbed the neighbors. He said, mischievously, "Shall we make a tent?"

"You mean right here?"

He nodded. "In the middle of the floor."

It was to be a tent in the middle of a forest and the light had to be dim (he turned them off and pulled the drapes) and, he added, peaceful (he actually turned off the stereo) because that was the way secret gardens and places were. He had read it in a book. He ran to the cupboard and began pulling out blankets and pillows, instructing me to help him move chairs and the couch so that we could hang blankets over them and make ourselves a rather odd sort of shelter, low and inviting, with an unzipped sleeping-bag to cushion us from the wool carpet. Soefi came sniffing over and immediately crawled inside and peered out at us. It was a kind of cloth cave, dark but not at all gloomy — a warm inviting space made from the clutter of a cupboard shelf.

He said that, before we entered, we had to take a vow to be best friends forever, even the cat. He pulled poor Soefi out by his front legs and held one paw aloft and made the thing promise. He was filled with the most marvellous energy, not at all manic or excited, to the brim but calm. I made the promise, hoping not to sound too solemn, and crawling on hands and knees followed him into our den. I thought perhaps the walls should have paintings of antelopes and bison. He lay on his back as I crawled in next to him, afraid to lift my head too far for fear of disturbing the ceiling of our precarious world.

He said, at one point, "I'm a fish. I have to lay on top of you and make my eggs come out."

"You don't have any," I said. He thought that was funny. His laughter only made his body tremble and slide all the more over me.

"You're getting all wet and huge," he said, looking down into my face.

Later he said, "Lie on top of me. We have to pretend we're in a war and bombs might fall on us and if you don't lie on top of me they'll get me." I lay on top of him and told him that I would protect him. He hugged me as hard as he could and pressed himself against me.

We showered together and wrapped ourselves in blankets, reluctant to dress. We sat on the floor at the opening of our tent eating our dinner and he said, quite out of the blue (I was not at all sure if he was serious or not): "If it gets inside of me then I'll get pregnant and have a baby and I'll be too young. I might have to put it up for adoption."

I started laughing and said, "Maybe it'll be twins."

He blushed. The blanket fell a bit off his shoulder. He leaned against me, "I can't really get pregnant." He played with my beard. Our faces were close.

"No," I said.

December 10th.

I have been telling Sander a thousand times that I love him, not to mention how many times I try to find out if he loves me. He makes fun of me when I go on like that, and it also annoys him. A few days ago — I suppose I had even been going on even more than usual — he handed me a sheet of lined school paper on which he had written laboriously five hundred times, 'I love you, I love you...' So I wouldn't keep asking him and going on about it he said. I imagined him spending the time at the desk in his room writing away, time after time, chuckling a little to himself. It pleased me very much. He made me pin it up on the wall of my study above my computer. His handwriting is neat and formal, the lines straight.

December 14th.

I was 'baby-sitting' Sander tonight, a term his mother uses casually, his father disdainfully, and I sometimes to tease. Since her exhibition last month Marijke has been socializing more than normally. Although the reviews were mixed there have been some sales and she seems to have managed to maintain her own identity and not be buried by the memory of her famous sculptor grandfather, or domineering photographer husband. The women's magazines have lauded the work's psychological depth, criticism of the modern family, view of the independent-minded woman. They have published two very good interviews with her and her comments on the current Dutch art scene have provoked some controversy. "It's a masculine jungle dominated by fourth-rate male egos." "Why aren't more women depicting more women?" She told me that she was enjoying all the attention.

Sander and I, still reading our Sherlock Holmes stories together, curled up on the couch. The originals are still a little too advanced for his level of English and we are using a simplified school version with full-page illustrations. He holds the book while I read. He had wrapped himself in one of those checkerboard, brown and orange, old-fashioned woolen bathrobes with white knotted cord belt such as I had not seen around since my early childhood. His well worn, faded blue flannel pajamas have a pattern of little white teddy bears; they are now a size too small for him, though not quite tattered enough to be discarded. He had the top buttoned all wrong, and it gaped askew: here and there a patch of taut skin visible. His legs are stretched out; the uncomfortably tight cloth had slid up above his ankles onto his calves. He was leaning back against me and I had one arm around him, awkwardly holding the book in front of us, letting him turn the pages. He had just showered; the back of his hair was still wet. He was fidgeting; raising his foot, dangling a furry tiger slipper from his big toe; twisting his foot to the side to see how far it would go without the slipper dropping off; raising his leg to see how high he could get it. He played with the cord of his pajama bottoms, pulling it out until the ends were even and then tying and untying it; twisted this way and that in my lap to get more comfortable; adjusted the book in front of us, running his hand over the hair on my arm pretending he was going to pull one out, but listened to every word of the story, even commenting on it as we went along. "That's stupid... What's he mean by that?... I would never do that."

We came to the end of a chapter and he jumped up and ran into the kitchen to get something to eat and drink. "Don't lose the place," he shouted. He came back into the living room balancing a tray laden with two glasses of coke, a big bowl of potato chips, cheese and crackers, chocolates, and roasted peanuts, and set it down very carefully on the coffee table. He sat next to me again, bending forward to reach for the food and drinks.

"Michiel's reading it too, but in Dutch," he said, obviously pleased with the fact that we were doing it in English. "He says it's boring and he can figure out the answer to the crime every time but I know he can't. He doesn't like this kind of story anyway."

"What does he like?"

He was still leaning over the table, stuffing himself full of junk food, but glancing at me back over his shoulder. "Crime stories, detectives, and girls and love, and stuff." A sharp nervous laugh erupted from him, and suddenly, eating something that went down the wrong way, he began to cough. I clapped him on the back. He gulped some cola and giggled again.

"What's so funny?"

"Nothing."

I pretended I was going to tickle him. "Come on, tell me."

He writhed this way and that. "I can't. It's a secret." He struggled free.

"I won't tell anyone. I promise."

"You will."

"Cross my heart. Pain of death."

It seems that an older cousin had traded some sex magazines for Michiel's old video games, and he had shown them to Sander. I still don't feel that I know Michiel all that well, although I've now met him six or seven times. He's a few months older than Sander, half a head taller, and looks older than eleven, so I wouldn't call him precocious. I asked Sander where he kept such things and it turned out he had a bizarre hiding place.

As Sander described it: "They have this old-fashioned bathroom — it's a really old house — and there's this wooden panel in the wall — in the bathroom I mean — behind where the toilet is — because there's pipes and things behind it — it's like a door, but not a door with a door knob, just screws he has to undo to get it off the wall you see, and be careful he doesn't lose any so he puts them in a little metal box because if he loses any his mother would see one was missing, and behind this sort of door, well it's not a door — a lid — there's like a hole or open space and he puts his magazines in a plastic bag and hides them behind the wall and you have to reach way in and up to get it — and there's insulation so you can get your arm itchy if you don't be careful — and if someone else takes the panel off they still can't see or find anything unless they know right where they have to reach up to get it."

He held up his fist in front of my face. "You promised not to tell, remember." I nodded. He was hunched forward, eating and drinking from the tray, and went on in the same vein: "He has photographs — really hot photographs so if his mother found out she would kill him if she knew what was there. You don't know her, she's sort of religious and goes to these weird church meetings and he only shows the stuff to me when no one's home, when his mother's out. She gets upset about everything. So he can only take it out when no one's around. Except me, I mean. And there's a few magazine, maybe six or seven, and photos — well, not really photos but sort of playing cards that are not playing cards when you look at them and they do everything in them and he even has condoms and boy they feel weird... " He suddenly stopped and glanced at me, but I did not say anything. "Really weird — Michiel's bigger than I am so his stays on. You should see, I mean he's lots bigger than mine. Lots." He turned to me and pretended to pout, and then glancing mischievously at me and narrowing his eyes, he held his hand far apart and said, "It's this big."

I had to laugh. "That sounds like a fish story. It can't be

that big."

"Oh yes it is, You should see it. Mine'll never be that big."

"So? He's probably just growing faster than you right now and you'll catch up with him."

He made a lewd, masturbatory gesture, which I took to mean something they did together, and then suddenly jumped up, nearly upsetting the tray and said, "I'm going for a piss." And dashed off to the bathroom. I looked at my watch. It was nearly ten. I put the book aside.

Later, as I was tucking him into bed he pointed across the room. I turned but wasn't sure what he meant. He pointed again but would not actually say what he wanted and I realized suddenly that he meant his teddy bear on the chair across the room. I fetched it and he took it from me, hugged it and curled up with it in his arms. I pulled the covers around his neck, and tucked in the edges. As I was leaving his room the images stayed in my mind: Sander cuddling with his bear; Sander trying on a condom and masturbating with Michiel; Sander and sex; Sander, sex and teddy bears. Somehow, I was not sure how, it all made sense.

3. Thursday Afternoon and Evening

I dozed off on Sander's bed, adrift in his nimbus. He and Michiel awakened me some minutes later, tumbling noisily into the house. I shouted down the stairs as I descended, "Shut up you two stupid little wild asses..." As I stepped off the bottom step Sander pounced on my back from behind the door jamb. "What have you two been up to?" I twirled him around and whiplashed him from side to side. He clung fiercely. I reached back and pinched him. He squealed, "I'll pull your beard!" I managed to dislodge him. "What were the two of you doing?" I asked with mock sternness.

"Buying cola, and stuff," Michiel said. He was standing to the side looking a little left out, grinning selfconsciously.

"It's party time," Sander said. "Cola, and chips, and cookies: come on!."

I admonished him: he was hyper enough without a dose of sugar; we were eating at six and I didn't want him to spoil his dinner. My parental tone dampened their spirits a bit and I regretted it. I would rather have lapsed into a lethean state of pure high-spirited boy-play. Adult reality was distant, formal, and stern.

I asked Michiel if he was staying for dinner. He rubbed his neck by his collar-bone, as if to draw attention to the fact that his shirt was open two or three buttons and he was not wearing an undershirt; tucked a lock of straight black hair behind his ear, scratched the corner of his eye. He was not particularly athletic but moved as someone confident of his body, not gangling as one would have supposed. He kept staring at me out of those haunting, pale blue eyes. If the two of us could somehow disembody, I thought, I would know what he was suggesting. He had to be home for dinner. I asked if he wanted me to call his mother and ask her if he could stay, but she was having a new boyfriend over and if he was not there she would think he did not like him.

"Do you?" I asked.

"He's all right. I mean, it has nothing to do with me. Mostly I'll only be in the way."

"Too bad for them," I said. He looked surprised, and then blushed.

They had not made much progress on their video school project. They wanted to do a teenage hero film, crime busters, dope smuggling, robots, and rescues. I said they should stick to something Dutch and stop thinking of Hollywood. Dutch, they said, was boring; Dutch was tulips and battles with floods — how could they film that? They were thinking: temples of doom, bat caves, cat women, laser rays taking out the bad guys. They hadn't filmed anything yet. We played a board game until Michiel had to leave.

I went into the kitchen to put the food in the oven and peel some potatoes; Sander followed. "Michiel really likes you," he said. I was pleased, but didn't want to be too obvious. "You know... at school today... You know what he did?"

Some bully had pushed Sander in the locker room and insulted him and Michiel had spontaneously come to his defense. This, and his earlier remark that he would 'punch someone out' for Sander's sake has totally proven to Sander that they were now bosom friends and he could count on him completely. Had Michiel intended it that way? "I can really trust him," he said. "We can tell each other anything." He slid up onto a stool at the counter and I started to mix a salad. "I even thought I'd tell him about — well — us, you know."

"I don't like people knowing about my private life. You know that," I said immediately, even a bit angrily.

I stopped what I was doing. This was out of the blue. What was going on? I certainly had mixed feelings. What was Sander's motive? Did he really mean to tell Michiel? Did I want Michiel to know? I had first to get my own thoughts clear: we had the right to keep some things private between us, and some things even were better left private, but I was not trying to dictate what he could or could not do. I could take that tack.

"Why do you want to tell him anyway? I mean what's private between us is private."

"Because we promised to tell each other everything. We swore an oath."

"When was that?"

"A couple of days ago. Honestly, we swore."

"Whose idea was that? Michiel's I bet."

"So? So what if it was?"

I thought Michiel's sexual curiosity might be directing itself into our lives.

"Well some things should be kept private between us. It's nobody's business except ours."

"Yeh, but I want to tell him."

I was not sure I understood whether he was feeling guilty or wanted to brag. I did have to admit to myself that it made me feel anxious. I was tempted to remind him of the previous summer, but I restrained myself. Instilling anxiety would not help anything.

I said, "Well, you know how I feel. What's private is private. Think it over carefully and let me know what you decide."

We left it that way, although now, as I think about it, I wonder if I was not being all too reasonable. Should I have taken an authoritarian stand and forbidden him to say anything? In any case I did not.

4. Thursday Late

It was nearly midnight before Marijke returned from giving her talk at the women's club. She said that it had gone quite well and that some women were going by the gallery to see whether they would buy watercolors. I gathered up my paraphernalia. Yes, Sander had gone to bed on time; he'd had a glass of milk and a story. I crammed clipboard, notes, books, and marking pens into my knapsack. She kept me lingering at the door, making small talk, blocking my exit. Her gray-streaked hair was pulled tightly back from her face giving it a kind of rigor and intensity that I found attractive. She lit a cigarette. Smoking fit her: the stern hair-do, the sharpness, her not-suffering-fools Dutchness.

She wanted to know how Sander had been, whether he and Michiel had gotten out of hand. I thought she wanted to talk about my friendship with him at this late hour, when I was tired and vulnerable, but she wanted to talk about Niek instead. Had I arranged to meet him at the gallery before the party on Saturday? I said I had.

She surprised me. "Well, I think that if he asks you, you should take over the gallery."

"Why? Is he going to ask me?"

"I don't know for sure. He hasn't said anything, but I suspect that's what he wants to talk about. You and I both know he's making a mess of it. Even he knows it! He's just too vain, or drunk half the time, to come right out and admit it."

"Yes, but why on earth would I want to take over the gallery?"

"Oh come now, you and I both know why. There's no sense in going around denying it. And you've been hinting at it for months."

"Well, if I have, then I wasn't aware of it."

"It's your contacts, and your sales that have been keeping us going. Niek is hardly there any more now that he's moved to the farm, and I don't want to be there either. Whether you'll admit it or not you like being there."

"Of course I do, but that is far short of taking it over. You and I know what the real financial situation is. There's hardly enough coming in to sustain expenses, let alone pay someone a living wage. I mean, if we didn't have help from all those volunteers it would have closed long ago."

"That's because Niek's no businessman. He gives away the photographs. If someone whines and says they don't have enough money he practically gives it to them for nothing. You know how he is. He should have never started a gallery in the first place. He's an idealist, not a businessman. That's not a criticism, it's just the way he is but that's not the type of person to run a gallery."

"Yes, but the real question is should anyone be running a photography gallery in the Netherlands. You know as well as I how dismal the situation is."

"Well, I could give you back your own arguments but I won't."

I had said often enough that the gallery had potential, that the photography market was international; there were, in fact, a few collectors to start with as a base; the museums would buy some work; we could sell drawings and maybe a few paintings as well.

I said, "I don't really see myself being a gallery director. I'm more the library type, sitting at a table with a bunch of reference works."

"I think you've only created that picture of yourself in order to finish your book. There are other sides to your personality too. What are you going to do then, leave Amsterdam? I don't think you really want to do that."

She was looking at me in a cool, detached way. I felt

quite uneasy. Nor did she relent: I would be good at it; she could see I was happy here; I would find it more challenging than teaching.

"That's all very well and good," I answered, backing out of the door a bit, "but he hasn't offered it to me yet and I'll wait and see what he says on Saturday."

As I was walking home I felt even more confused than I felt a couple of days before. Stay here, or leave Sander behind? I didn't want to think about any of it. I didn't want to go and see Niek either now that I more or less knew what it was going to be about. I was angry with all of them. But why was I angry?

Part Four: Toon's Trial

1. Friday, March 2nd

I was up early this morning in order to be at the court house at nine for Toon's trial. It started at ten but some people were meeting in the foyer for coffee before going up to the visitors' balcony.

A very odd thing happened. The new courthouse in Amsterdam South is quite far from my house and I left the house just after eight so that a brisk walk in the cold morning air would wake me up. As I was nearing the building, a huge, sterile grey, cement thing they have attempted to decorate with bilious blue tiles, and was starting up the car ramp to the front door, the architect having conveniently omitted a sidewalk, I saw Toon ahead of me just about to enter the building. Dressed in a long, grey-blue raincoat, he was stooped over and walking with a cane, looking like some dark, foreboding, Dostoievskian figure: sour, glum, and ashen. He banged the cane against the ground; it echoed resoundingly from the walls of the lifeless building. His rage seemed to have taken him over. I had never seen him with a cane, perhaps his lawyer had advised it for effect, but it brought out his dark side. When I entered the ugly foyer with its plastic plants and hollow sounds I felt like returning home and might have had there not been a group of people there that I knew, and had not Dr Born come over to greet me.

I joined them: Matt, an American expatriate and now a Dutch citizen, and Wim, a Dutch acquaintance and photographer, were talking to Toon's lawyer.

"Erich," I said, shaking his hand. "Pleasant surprise. The mountain come to Mohammed. I thought I wouldn't see you until later?"

"Will. How could I miss your performance today as 'expert witness'. You know, I think the role suits you." He did not appear to be disdainful.

I asked, "What do you think will be the outcome?"

"The outcome is clear, isn't it? The sentence is the only real discussion, and that will depend on whether the prosecutor tries to make a monster of him or not, doesn't it? And lately, they always do."

"So you think he'll get the maximum? A year or two years?"

"Well, Will, this is the Netherlands you know. And then, there's the circumstance of his sick father. The court likes that sort of thing. A sick parent being taken care of by a dutiful son. At most they might give him a suspended sentence."

"Is that your prediction? That wouldn't be too bad."

Matthew had come over to join us and disagreed. The Dutch were getting just as bad as the Americans, and he thought that Toon would get at least a year and maybe even two. He added a fact I had not heard before, that some of the Amsterdam morals squad had been trained recently at the FBI center in New York. That was proof enough that they were all just becoming American, and that everything would be getting, if it was not already, worse and worse.

Erich said, "My God, Matthew, I didn't realize you were such a pessimist."

Matt and Wim edited the Dutch paedophile movement magazine, called for some obscure reason that no one seemed to know, *Robijn* — perhaps (as Wim speculated) because that had been the name of someone's boy friend at the time of its founding. I met them now and again on a social basis: for movies, or a dinner, to gossip and share news. I also wrote reviews for their magazine under another name. They had been trying to get me to be on the staff. I kept saying I was too busy and kept a bit apart, mostly to protect the privacy of my relationship with Sander. They had met him once, one evening as we were coming out of a movie theater and they were just going in. We stopped to chat. Sander was restless. He wanted to eat and I did not linger. Matt phoned the following day, obviously to find out who Sander was, but I did not offer him any information.

Erich was the only person who knew the whole story

about Sander. I said to him, "You seem to be in a good mood today."

"I always am when I see you, Will."

I thought, Erich is in one of his impervious moods. His long thin, dyed black hair was slicked back straight off his forehead, making him a little forbidding. He asked me, "Do you share our friend's pessimism about the American influence?"

I said, "In general the discussion here has been more rational than in the US or England. I probably would go along with you that Toon will get six months suspended sentence because of his father. If it were the US they would give him forty years and force the father into an underfunded state home." I added, "After all they've already made an exception for his father. They've let him stay out of jail during the trial." Toon had a small row house in Amsterdam North and had moved his sick father in with him despite his own incapacity. The Dutch are a very family-conscious society. Toon had only one older brother who was a bad painter involved in Eastern religions, and lived in a messy, subsidized studio out in the eastern dock district; he'd had several breakdowns and was completely irresponsible. Toon (and the state) saw it as his family duty to take in his father.

Wim added to the discussion. He had seen an obscure government report that gave the names of the two morals police that had been trained by the FBI. He said, "You know what a perverse, hate-ridden document the FBI manual is. And what they think of paedophiles — devils incarnate! Give it another year or two and that will be the attitude here. Look at the sentences recently. They have been going up. I agree with Matt."

Erich said, a little harshly I thought, that it was useless to argue perceptions. Predictions were parlor games; the words pessimism and optimism when it came to paedophilia had no meaning; proofs lay in hard historical analysis. But I thought to myself, well they are just talking, venting steam. I said I needed coffee and, as we went into the cafeteria, I saw that monster of a social worker, Lucy, who had caused all the trouble for Toon, sitting across the room with the prosecutor. She was wearing an attractive, light-blue print dress with a pale salmon-colored sweater thrown over her shoulders, and I'll have to say in her favor, her clothes suited her quite well. She certainly has neurotic mannerisms though: she was speaking rapidly and using a lot of hand gestures, which was not very Dutch; she bit her thumbnail, and groped for something in her handbag, spilling some papers on the floor. She looked around nervously, and I could see she was irritating the prosecutor.

I felt my prejudices boiling over. I have I admit a tendency to affix the same detestable characteristics to all social workers: they do more harm than good; they are all sexually ignorant; they are trying to reinforce our misunderstandings and ignorance of sexuality by repressive application of harmful laws that are disastrous to human lives; they are intractable social fundamentalists who feel they serve the truth and protect children when they perpetrate their own form of abuse by distorting children's reality. I view them mostly as the front persons for society's sexual guilt, the advance guard of sexual suppression.

Over coffee I learned a few more facts from Matt and Wim about Lucy's role in the Toon affair. It was not all bad, of course. She had been trying to find work for Ashok's father, and as Ashok's mother was pregnant again she was also trying to make sure that the family had the proper balanced diet, that the shopping got done and Ashok and his sister fed. That meant that she was around their apartment several times a week and also that she had assumed a kind of authoritarian role in the family. Doing good is a convenient mask for autocracy.

Toon had been trying to time his own visits to Ashok's in such a way as to avoid her, but he had cultivated the practice of doing certain things with the family to keep good communication between them, such as joining them for an occasional Sunday outing. Ashok's grades were not very good and Toon went to their apartment once a week to help him with math and Dutch. Lucy usually dropped by unannounced, perhaps deliberately. The first time they were introduced she was very friendly, but the second time she asked a few curt questions and the third time she took out a cigarette, sat down nervously at the kitchen table, and hovered around menacingly.

There was a confrontation between them soon afterwards. Toon and Ashok were doing the family shopping and had just come out of the supermarket when they met her in the plaza. She said she wanted to see him at her office to discuss Ashok and could they make an appointment right then and there. He deferred a bit, saying something about not having his appointment book with him (the Dutch live by their agendas), more or less putting her off. She snapped at him (according to him at least) that he had better come to her office to see her at nine the next morning. Toon became stubborn and said he had to be at work in the morning. She flared up: she knew all about him and if he didn't show up she'd take steps.

He argued. He insisted that there wasn't much to say, he was a friend of the family and was just helping out by doing the shopping; he would be wasting her office time by coming by; he was sorry she might be in a bad mood but he didn't see that she could object to his being a family friend because after all right now the family needed some outside help as she well knew. And then he made a mistake. He flatly refused to go and see her. He had not taken in the fact that she had power over him.

Something later happened that I have mulled over a great deal. When the police searched his apartment they found nude photographs of Ashok that Toon had failed to remove from his house despite his knowing there was an ongoing investigation. Some were very incriminating. What made him overlook such a thing? Perhaps those who act outside the law, even from conscience, strike an odd sort of tension between the inner authority of their own personality and the external authority of the law. It is too easy to say that Toon wanted to be caught; or punished. He might have wanted a fight, a conflict with authority, a challenge he might hope to win. He was very angry and defiant. The conventional view is that authority figures trigger our guilt, no matter how slight or serious our offense, and we therefore seek to expunge it. Some people might see tests of authority as expressions of freedom.

Then, suddenly, there was Toon walking slowly through the cafeteria with his lawyer. He was near enough for me to see beads of sweat on his forehead. Perhaps he was in pain today from his leg or back. I turned to see if Lucy was watching and I saw that she and the prosecutor both were. I went over and wished him success. He said cynically, "Not much chance of that."

I did not stop to argue. The others were at the cash register and I went to pay for my coffee. The thought ran through my mind, "What if this were me on trial for Sander?" What, I wondered, made Toon so dark to me; was it that his sense of self was being threatened, that very thing that allowed him to love Ashok? Was it this the prosecution would attack, distort, and attempt to destroy?

2. Brooding

The observers' balcony had the appearance of a movie theater — tiered, numbered rows of red, upholstered seats; with one exception, the front was not open, but enclosed by a sliding glass wall. We were among the first there and sat in the front row, behind the glass. The balcony was sloped in such a way (deliberately?) that we could only see the front half of the courtroom where the principals sat. Press and witnesses sat at the back, but crane as I might I could not see who was at that end of the room. According to Toon's lawyer, I was not supposed to be called until the afternoon, and so I had joined the others in the balcony for the morning.

It was extremely hot. We tried to open the glass panels but they were locked. A guard walked into the courtroom below and I rapped politely on the glass with a key. He ignored it. Wim, not one to mince about, banged loudly. The guard turned and was going to ignore us but Wim pounded more loudly still and gestured. The guard waved angrily, which seemed to mean he was coming.

I removed my jacket and sweater, and sank back in the seat. I didn't feel like saying much. I kept thinking of Sander, and the vulnerability of the relationship. After all, what guarantee did I have that some child-protection social worker wouldn't do the same to Sander and me? Or perhaps I would have trouble with Marijke again, though things were calm between us now. Did she want me to take over the gallery from Niek so that I could show her work? I felt guilty for thinking that. After all, she had a gallery, even if she had personality clashes with the director. What had she said, something about my 'missing Sander'? Surely she was above using Sander to receive something from me. The atmosphere of the trial must be causing crazy thoughts. Or fear.

If I had asked Toon he would have said cynically that he was sure it was only a matter of time before someone interfered with Sander and me. Perhaps one of Sander's teachers seeing me one day meeting him outside the Montessori school might ask him about me and begin to wonder. Anything could happen, he would say. Realities in our world were fragile, relationships tentative.

Of course, my circumstances were different. Sander's family was not in the same position as Ashok's family. There were no social workers hovering about the house butting into Marijke's affairs. She was prosperous, not just from Niek's payments, but from family money as well. The house on the Oude Waal had been inherited. I could not imagine Marijke putting up with Lucy for one minute.

Still questions had been asked. Marijke's elder sister had already wondered about Sander and me. She had been visiting one day when I stopped by to pick up Sander for a movie and had immediately started cross-examining and insinuating. She knew I was a 'consultant' at the gallery but Marijke reported that she asked her, "Will hangs around an awful lot with Sander, and I've never seen him at any openings with a woman." Marijke said I was a special friend of the family, that is, one who washes the dishes, walks the dog and takes the children to films and carnivals.

Other people were coming into the balcony and Dr Born was trying to draw me into a conversation. I turned around to see if any others had entered whom I knew. To my surprise about thirty people had filed in while I was brooding.

Erich was telling me about another case he had heard of recently. He was going to be an expert witness. A twelve-year-old boy had been arrested for having sex with 260 different age-mates over an eighteen-month period, as it had been reported by the police. I laughed. It was statistically absurd to think that a boy as young as ten and a half could find more than two and half different children per week to 'abuse'. Children that age just did not have that range of contacts. It didn't make sense at all, and yet it was being taken quite seriously. More sexual hysteria. I pointed out to Erich that it also admitted that young children could have powerful sex drives.

The guard we had seen below came in with a key and with a considerable amount of fuss managed to open the huge sliding windows.

Toon entered behind his lawyer. He settled into his seat but the cane fell on the floor and as he began to stoop over, the prosecutor bent and picked it up. By leaning far forward I could just see the middle of the room below. Ashok's mother was there, sitting next to Lucy. The atmosphere almost seemed bizarrely friendly, though the formal black robes of the lawyers, and the pale gray and blue decor, the wood-panelled hushed room, reminded one just enough of the reality.

Erich said to me, "You're very quiet all of a sudden."

I looked at my watch. It was already ten-fifteen. I said that I was not quite awake yet. But I was thinking of Sander. Sometimes, no one else existed except us, and nothing could in any way interfere with us. There, in the courtroom, that thing I called simply loving Sander seemed a tentative thing. I had to ask myself the question if, out of love, I was not ethically bound to end the relationship to spare him even the possibility of such legal repercussions as the one I was about to witness. I knew that Ashok had been questioned not just once but several times and the thought of Sander going through such a thing nearly made me sick. I thought I really should leave; just go back to my secure job and in a year or two tenure. I felt suffocated by the room; the whole thing was making me paranoid.

3. Morning Session

Dutch trials are conducted before a three-judge tribunal with no jury. They entered the room and we all stood. The chief judge was an attractive woman in her thirties. Even from where I was sitting I could see that she was wearing eye shadow. She had, I thought, a pleasant, intelligent face. She said something to her colleagues that must have amused them because they laughed. My spirits lifted a bit. She seemed reasonable. Perhaps Toon had a chance.

But then Wim leaned over and said, "Bad news; she's a real bitch."

I looked again. She was scrutinizing us, a frown on her face. She leaned over and passed some instruction to the court guard standing closest to the bench. For a moment everyone below — judges, lawyers, even Toon — turned to stare up at the gallery. I supposed she disapproved of the procedure of opening the glass wall. The guard disappeared out a side door and in just a couple of minutes he was in the balcony telling us that the judge would allow the windows to remain open only if we kept absolutely silent. Two men I knew from one of the gay rights groups said very loudly that they considered such advise condescending and unwelcome. The judge's face remained impassive. Did she expect a demonstration, I wondered?

The trial began with the usual procedures and shuffling of papers. I had learned some things about Dutch law from Dr Born. Prosecutions were usually not brought before the court unless the investigation had yielded strong evidence of guilt. In fact, only about ten per cent of all trials here resulted in acquittals. In those that did the defendant could file to recoup his costs, which was thought of as a deterrent to bringing weak cases with only circumstantial evidence. One might say that in Dutch trials the person is nether considered innocent until proven guilty, nor the reverse. The presupposition might be, however, that someone is likely guilty, though this is a simplification. For example, there is a procedure to appeal the prosecution itself before trial.

In Toon's case, unfortunately, the possibility of acquittal seemed to me even slighter than ten per cent. Besides the unfortunate remark by Ashok's mother to Lucy about their sleeping naked together, there were the nude photographs, and Ashok's statement to the police that Toon had performed certain acts on him. This the defense would challenge by asserting that the police had extracted a confession. Toon had admitted to nothing. Ashok was only eight at the time the alleged sex started and the courts treated that more seriously than had he been twelve or fourteen, and more capable of consent. The trial would also revolve around two issues: whether there had been force, or 'rape' as defined by the law, that is, whether the specific kind of sexual acts had been penetrative or not. Penetrative acts carried much higher sentences.

The prosecution was also trying to complicate the case by introducing the matter of the photographs. There were two that were especially in question: in one Ashok was lying on a bed and clearly displayed an erection. Toon had superimposed in the background a male nude figure by a window wearing artificial wings, a kind of Duane Michaels clone photograph, and had titled it 'Boyhood Desire'. The other was in the style of Edward Weston's Neil nudes and showed Ashok's midriff, also with the beginnings of an erection. It was titled 'Weston Aroused'. Toon had exhibited both photographs in a Dutch gay gallery and at a gay arts festival in Berlin, along with adult male and female nudes. They had also been published in Wim and Matt's paedophile magazine, and in a couple of the gay and lesbian magazines, hence the presence and interest of some members of the gay community. I was to testify that they had artistic merit, in spite of, or because of, their erotic edge; in my judgement the artist's intention was not exploitative. The prosecution, of course, claimed they had no artistic merit and were pornographic. They had also found multiple copies of them, and claimed that Toon was therefore guilty of the production and distribution of child pornography. If he was found guilty under a separate statute this would also carry a high sentence.

As much as I could follow the technical Dutch of the trial with Dr Born's help, the prosecutor was basing his case not on proving Toon's guilt, but on establishing that emotional coercion and violence had been done to Ashok, and warranted therefore the highest penalty. Bribery disguised as gifts was intended to coax sexual favors from Ashok. If Toon's intentions were solely exploitative and sexual, then the photographs also became tainted.

The matter came up quickly, perhaps only a half hour into the proceedings. Dutch judges are allowed to question the defendant, and at one point the chief judge asked him if he had given Ashok any money for sex and Toon had firmly denied it.

JUDGE: But surely you gave him money?

TOON: Yes.

JUDGE: How much did this come to?

TOON: (thinking for a moment) I gave him ten guilders now and then to go to the store to buy candy, soda and chips for a little party.

JUDGE: Ten guilders is a lot of money to a small child. Did he give you back the change?

TOON: No, I let him keep it, but it was usually only a guilder or less, for running the errand.

JUDGE: How often did you have these parties?

TOON: Once or twice a month.

JUDGE: (writing something down) And you bought him clothing, and even a bicycle?

TOON: Yes. For school.

JUDGE: An expensive mountain bike. (Rifling through her papers.) And, expensive sports shoes, a wristwatch, a Walkman, clothes. It's a long list.

TOON: He needed things for school. The family couldn't afford it. I always asked his mother's permission first.

The prosecutor followed the same line of questioning.

He was tall and thin and much younger than Toon's lawyer, wore horn-rimmed glasses and seemed nervous and uncertain of himself. He cleared his throat and when he asked his first question his voice was shaky. He drank a sip of water.

PROSECUTOR: Did his mother know you were buying these things in exchange for sexual favors?

Toon's lawyer objected, but Toon insisted on answering.

TOON: I wasn't. There was no exchange.

PROSECUTOR: Just gifts (pause). And sex. Separated. Like that. Gifts over there. Sex way over there. No connection whatsoever.

TOON: Children of nine, ten don't have their own money in this society. There is no way they can get it either. I asked him to do work for me so he could get an allowance. He washed the dishes and took the dog for walks. Things like that. He certainly couldn't get the things he needed from his parents.

The matter at that point was dropped, and I breathed a sigh of relief that was only short-lived. A few minutes later, upon cross-examination, it came back to the same subject.

TOON'S LAWYER: Ashok's family... They were poor? On welfare?

TOON: Yes.

LAWYER: They couldn't buy things for him that other families bought for their children: bicycles and such?

TOON: No.

LAWYER: You asked their permission.

TOON: Yes. We had a general understanding. At the beginning, when I first knew Ashok I asked permission each time, but then I asked if it was all right and they said it was. They were glad. They couldn't do it themselves.

The judge intervened again.

JUDGE: Did you buy things for the rest of the family? (Consulting her papers again.) There's a younger sister I see. Did you buy things for her, or for his mother or father?

TOON: Yes. Sometimes.

JUDGE: What for example?

TOON: Once, when his father had a job interview I bought him a white shirt and a tie. Mostly it was gifts though for Christmas or birthdays or holidays.

JUDGE: But with Ashok it was more frequent. Not just for special occasions?

TOON: Yes.

JUDGE: How often do you think? Including sodas, candy and more expensive things too. How often do you think this would have been?

TOON: I tried to arrange it so that he had some of his own money. He had an allowance and I tried to teach him to carry money. I bought him a change purse. But he lost it. When he took out his handkerchief he would drop money; lose it. Things like that. So, I gave up because he would get upset and cry when he lost his money. So I carried it for him.

JUDGE: The question was, how often?

TOON: I would think, if you include everything, every third or fourth time we were together.

Children, of course, did not have money of their own. It was a specious line of questioning somewhere out of reality, though it was clear what they were trying to prove: that Toon had coerced, bribed Ashok into sexual acts; that he had bought Ashok's affection, bought Ashok's way into his bed. But, children did not have their own money. That is the way society worked. They received it from adults. If Toon had forced Ashok to do heavy work in exchange for pay he could have been tried under other laws. I felt angry. The real issue was sex. Without it this transference of goods between adult and child would not have been used to prove abuse. The sex was coloring the exchange, to be sure, though I wondered if Toon had not overdone his gifts.

I had done more or less the same with Sander: bought him ice creams, sodas, hamburgers, french fries. How often had I paid for his dinner, for a movie, bought gifts for him when I was away on business, even a sweater once when we were shopping together, on an impulse because white made him look so attractive? I hadn't given it much thought. Perhaps that was wrong; perhaps I should have. It had all seemed perfectly normal to me at the time, a kind of overflowing of affection. Sometimes was I being too sentimental, a little sappy about him, thinking of what a sweet smile he would have when he opened the box? Once, when in Berlin doing research at the state library, I had brought him back a Russian camera someone was selling on the street that cost only a few dollars. I had bought it on an impulse, thinking it was so cheap that even if he threw it away it wouldn't matter too much. He could use it when we went on vacations, or camping. He had liked it immensely. Yet, suddenly, here in this courtroom all those gifts and treats and movies and the camera were being trotted out as coercion. How complicated it all was. As if there were an unwritten law, "Thou shalt beware of giving gifts to a child who is not your own." Yet, parents bought their children's affection too, or grandparents, or aunts and uncles. When money or goods was coupled with sex, there was not much defense one could muster against it; the link automatically made it black. The prosecution (or, I might have said, 'society') was trying to prove that the money represented abuse, Toon that it represented caring. Two conflicting realities were clashing.

PROSECUTOR: Was it necessary to give the boy everything you gave him?

TOON: No, not a necessity.

PROSECUTOR: Yet you gave it.

TOON: We were out biking or walking and there was the ice-cream so we stopped and bought something. It just happened.

PROSECUTOR: And you always paid?

TOON: Yes.

PROSECUTOR: So you gave him everything he wanted and spent all this money on him.

TOON: Not everything he wanted. Sometimes I said no.

PROSECUTOR: But the boy knew when he was with you he would get a lot of treats, that it was worthwhile hanging around you, so when you wanted sex he must have thought that he had better give you what you wanted. After all, you were taking care of him, buying him all these things.

An objection again from Toon's lawyer. The prosecution had not established that sexual acts had taken place.

TOON: I tried to teach Ashok that he always had a choice. I was careful to try to instill this.

PROSECUTOR: (sarcastically) Oh, you talked about it. You said he had choices, but you lavished him with gifts? Did you stop for a while giving him things to see whether he would still be your friend, take a rest from it for a few weeks, even as an experiment?

TOON: No.

PROSECUTOR: You just kept on giving.

TOON: I didn't see any need to stop.

PROSECUTOR: So, you were out and about together, and buying him this and that and then you would go back to your house and want sex with him, and it doesn't sound as if the boy had much choice.

Toon's lawyer interrupted.

LAWYER: It has already been established that there was an exchange of money and goods in this relationship. The defendant was in the habit of helping this family, and this child, financially. Now, the testimony of the boy himself states, "I did not do anything I did not want to do." We have heard the defendant himself say that he went out of his way to explain this to the child. We also know that the mother did not object to the friendship. So perhaps we can get to the point of the prosecutor's questions.

PROSECUTOR: The point is that the defendant was signalling the child to have sex with him; that he ingratiated himself with the family in order to abuse this boy and used money to confuse the family and exert power over them in order to insure their silence. Money was only an instrument of power. The boy saw it as affection. The defendant did untold violence and harm to this boy by using gifts to distort affection.

I held my breath. This was a crucial point. The judge rifled through her papers and, putting on, and taking off, her reading glasses she said to the prosecutor: "I do not in the indictment see any mention of physical force or forced entry of the boy, or any mention of any other kind of physical violence." She put the paper down and folded her hands. "Are you contending that there was such in this case?"

PROSECUTOR: We are only contending that there was psychological violence.

JUDGE: Then there is no evidence whatsoever of physical violence or rape?

PROSECUTOR: No.

At that point she directed a few more questions at Toon, and again all I could think of was that realities were again diverging. They were, I thought, strange, surreal questions.

JUDGE: If this matter of sex with children were to become legal, would you still love them in the same way?

Dr Born whispered to me, "What a bizarre question. He had better answer carefully." I was not sure what she was after but I remembered Dr Born's advice that you act humbly in court and say things like, "Yes, Your Honor, I definitely need therapy and want to change." This seemed like a tricky way of asking the same.

TOON: (hesitating) Can you repeat the question. I'm not sure I understood it.

She repeated the question verbatim.

TOON: By 'loving them the same way' do you mean sexually?

JUDGE: Yes.

TOON: Yes, I think I would. I mean... at least... I'm not sure.

He glanced at his lawyer and seemed confused.

JUDGE: Yes or no?

TOON: Yes.

Her question made me angry. It was clear to me what she was after: forbidden fruit tasted sweeter. It was not love motivating the man to have sex with the child but lust for the forbidden, the defiance of moral and legal strictures. I mean, what on earth did she think, that men had gone around loving boys for thousands of years only because it was illegal! The question was completely duplicitous, because what she really wanted to know was whether Toon intended to change his behavior. His 'yes' now indicated that he thought his desires were innate. To make matters worse, at least in my mind worse, she now made one of the most bizarre statements I had so far heard.

JUDGE: If you were willing to get rid of your desire your life would be a lot simpler. That desire has led to your arrest.

Someone behind me immediately booed very loudly, and someone else stamped their feet. She glanced up at us angrily. I felt like throwing something. I saw her glance around for the court clerk, but the noise died down immediately.

4. Afternoon Session

By the lunch recess I felt that some of it at least had been civil and routine — with an absence of the kind of inflammatory rhetoric that pervaded the American and English courts. The prosecutor had not tried to depict Toon as a folk devil, nor had he claimed Toon was the vilest monster that had ever walked the earth, as might have been said in an Anglo-American courtroom. Wim was of another opinion. He thought the judge's tone had been pretty hostile. I felt that my Dutch was not good enough to catch subtleties and connotations. Dr Born had been to so many of these for so many years that he saw nothing extraordinary in this one, which, I felt, was exceptional in a way. The Dutch might be influenced by hysterias temporarily but the trial had the air of business as usual.

The afternoon session at first did not add much to the morning's proceedings. I was now told by Toon's lawyer that I should sit downstairs at the back of the courtroom, and found myself just behind Lucy. She was the first person called that afternoon, and I have to say that she kept to the facts. Officials, when in an official setting faced with other officials, generally behave themselves.

We all had thought that Ashok's mother would be called, but despite references to statements in the depositions that she had made she was not called to the stand. Suddenly it was my turn. I walked nervously to the front of the room. They had an interpreter waiting. I could not make notes of the dialogues as I had done before but as best as I can remember this is what happened. I stated my credential, Associate Professor, Art Department, San Francisco State University, author of this and that on photography.

PROSECUTOR: You are also friends with the defendant?

ME: Yes.

Several photographs of Toon's were brought out and shown to the court. There was a pause while they were circulated between the judges. The two I had thought would be the most dubious were indeed the focus of the questioning, but I hoped I had prepared myself.

PROSECUTOR: Would you say that the boy in these photographs is clearly exhibiting an erection?

ME: No. I would not necessarily say that.

PROSECUTOR: Surely you can see that the penis is pointing up and exhibits every indication of an erection?

ME: I would say that the photographer intends to suggest an erection but that there is some flaccidity in the organ. In reading a photograph you have to take account of every element in order to determine the photographer's intention. If he had intended to show an erection unequivocally he would have done that. But he has not, so I take it to mean he had other intentions.

PROSECUTOR: What are these other intentions?

ME: Humor first of all. I think the photographs are humorous comments about other photographs commonly known in the history of photography. These two photographs make a joke about other work. For example, the photograph entitled 'Weston Aroused' I think criticizes Edward Weston for suppressing Neil's sexuality and making Neil into a plastic, neo-Grecian statue, which is strange for a father to do with his son. The photograph restores the sexuality to the boy, Ashok, but that does not make it pornographic. I think it is rich in associations.

PROSECUTOR: Would you call it an erotic work?

ME: To me it is not. It is too detached and objective, too

filled with puns and irony. I think the partly erect penis, even the fact that the boy depicted is not middle-class white as was Neil, create too many meanings to make a simple label possible. The Indian-Surinamese boy restores the sexuality lost by the American boy. Now the other photograph with the nude angel clearly refers to a famous Duane Michaels photograph. Here I think the intention is to link photos of boys to photos of men, to link the gay and paedophile concerns. Toon (I used his last name) is creating a myth with Ashok, just as Michaels creates a myth. The boy is experiencing homosexual desire. His erotic fantasy is of the handsome angel-man floating through his bedroom window, perhaps even into his bed. It is as absurd to call this work pornographic as it is to say that the smile on the Mona Lisa's face was meant by da Vinci to suggest orgasm (laughs from the gallery). Art deals with enigmas and these photographs are enigmatic, as is, I might add, paedophile, or gay, or heterosexual desire.

I did not say too much more and as I walked towards the back of the room I recognized a gallery owner I knew who sold some homoerotic work. He was obviously also going to appear as an expert witness. I decided to go upstairs and join the others, as I was not appearing on the stand again. I stopped for coffee first and by the time I settled in an empty seat next to Erich, Toon was being called once more. I have to say that his questioning this time was for me even more bizarre.

Dr Born had told me he had met with Toon the previous week and gone over the trial procedure with him. He was still a licensed, though retired, psychotherapist, and had advised a lot of people on the psychology of courts and the best strategy for testifying. He said that Toon was quite resistant to his advice and we were both concerned that he would be hostile on the stand. Erich's theory was that preaching a militant, sexual revolutionary attitude antagonized the court and only caused higher sentences. His advice was to act like a good Calvinist, be repentant, talk about caring for his father, give the impression of being a good son, and also say that he was getting psychological help for his 'problem'. If he did all those things, as there were extenuating circumstances, he would almost certainly receive a suspended sentence. Toon, however, who was obviously angry, said that he would not bend over for the courts and would uphold his 'God-given right' to have a relationship with Ashok. If he did that his militancy would signal to the court an 'asocial' attitude threatening to children and leave them with no alternative but to jail him. Erich's point was that a cry for personal freedom would be ironically self-destructive and counter-productive, and he should take a pragmatic approach. Toon wanted nothing to do with that.

We waited with baited breath as Toon stood in the aisle next to his chair to answer questions. He leaned on his cane and spoke slowly, though forcefully. Neither the prosecutor nor the judge was antagonistic; the questioning, at first, was pretty much a rehash of the morning's procedures. But then the prosecutor, consulting his notes, brought up the sexual side of the relationship and began to read from Ashok's deposition descriptions of sexual acts that had allegedly taken place and could be construed under the law as 'penetrative'. If he established 'penetrative' acts, and bribery and coercion as well, Toon could indeed receive a high sentence. Penetrate meant an act in which any part of the body was entered, orally or anally. As far as I knew there was no proof of any of this against Toon. The prosecutor, standing by his own chair and facing Toon, read out a series of statements and descriptions that Ashok had made.

PROSECUTOR: Ashok Rahman's deposition states that 'he put his mouth on my penis about ten times'. Is this true?

TOON: No.

PROSECUTOR: He states that 'he rubbed my penis up and down and did it until it made me feel all funny lots of time, most always when we were in bed together and I couldn't go to sleep and it made me sleepy', and that you did this according to the statement 'a hundred times or so'. Is that true?

TOON: No.

PROSECUTOR: The boy further states 'he liked to wash me in the bathtub and take showers together and he put soap on my cock and squeezed it and he washed me all over even on my behind with his hand and showed me how to keep my hole clean'. Is this true?

Erich nudged me. The questioning was on thin ice.

TOON: Boys get smelly and don't always wash properly, so I did wash him in my bathtub.

PROSECUTOR: Isn't this odd, washing a boy in that particular area.

TOON: Boys are careless about hygiene.

PROSECUTOR: The boy said, 'he washed me all around there and showed me how...' Well, I don't have to read it again. Wasn't your purpose something more than hygiene?

TOON: No. He didn't keep himself clean and I was teaching him how to wash. He didn't know the first thing.

PROSECUTOR: And you didn't intend something else to happen once he understood it felt good?

TOON: No.

PROSECUTOR: It is also in the testimony that you forced him to masturbate you several times.

Toon's lawyer interrupted: The deposition does not say 'forced'.

TOON: I never used force with Ashok about anything, even brushing his teeth. That was the worst, brushing his teeth.

PROSECUTOR: The boy states, 'I touched his thing and rubbed it and stuff came out.' Is this true?

TOON: Mostly we cuddled. He's very affectionate.

PROSECUTOR: The boy states, 'He put oil on my thing and all around and even on my hole and then he rubbed me and I had a big thrill.' Is this accurate?

TOON: Sometimes I gave him massages. He plays soccer and gets aching muscles. I think he plays too much soccer, but there is all this pressure on him at school because he is so good at it. I think the pressure is terrible, a kind of abuse. I even went and talked to the school about it.

PROSECUTOR: And, of course, with no further intentions.

TOON'S LAWYER: Objection. If my colleague wishes to cite something in the record that points to some other fact, then let him cite the record.

PROSECUTOR: It seems from the testimony that you abused this boy and otherwise put him in jeopardy under very odd circumstances. For example, is it not true that once, on a trip to one of the northern islands 'he sucked my thing in the toilet on the ferryboat and someone knocked on the door and I got scared'?

TOON: We were on the ferryboat and he had to go to the toilet and he was frightened to go in there alone in case the ship sunk. I don't know, but he had a lot of anxiety that day. I'm not sure why.

PROSECUTOR: Further the boy states, 'once he put his tongue in my mouth'. Is this true?

TOON: I don't remember ever doing that.

Erich leaned over to say that French kissing was a grey area of the law. It was technically 'penetrative' if by the adult.

PROSECUTOR: And the boy says, 'He put his tongue in my mouth and on my hole and made it go around and around and he did that a lot because he liked to do that and at first I thought it was funny but I liked it when he put his tongue in my mouth and made it go around and around and rubbed my thing.'

TOON: I remember Ashok got some kind of sex comic book from a friend of his and it talked a lot about using the tongue.

I saw the judge making notes. French kissing. A basic act of intimacy? Sander did not like to kiss. Yet, what if this one fact, technically a 'penetrative act', resulted in a twelve-year sentence for Toon? I leaned over and said this to Dr Born. He whispered, "If this is all they have I doubt whether it will lead to a severe sentence."

I had been distracted and had lost the train of the proceedings, but when I concentrated again I realized that the judge was correcting the prosecutor. She had said something about not being sure of the direction of the questioning but that if there was some evidence of force or violence in this relationship she would like to hear it. As there was not, could they move on to other things. As we were leaving I said to Erich, "How odd that trials have become one of the few events where child sexuality is so openly and pornographically described."

Erich said, "They even were in the eighteenth century. It's a rather odd way we have of admitting a reality."

5. Dinner with Erich Born

The trial was over at about five o'clock; the verdict and sentencing would be in another two weeks. There was a good deal of disagreement among us about what it would be, but I ended up agreeing with Dr Born's suggestion that Toon would perhaps be forced into therapy but would not be jailed. His sick father, I seconded, gave the Dutch court an irresistible opportunity to show its humanity. Neither Wim nor Matt shared our optimism.

Erich and I found a small Turkish restaurant near the courthouse, the others would join us later at the paedophile workgroup meeting where we would also be able to learn from Toon his lawyer's reaction to the trial. The waiter came to take our order and Erich said something in Turkish that seemed to frighten the man. I asked him what he had said and it was simply, "The weather is cold in Amsterdam but in Ankara it is warm." Perhaps the man had thought it was some code and that Erich was the secret police? We laughed, which did not entirely improve my mood. We were the only people there. Our table was covered with an old-fashioned, red and white checked oilcloth I had not seen in use since my childhood. There were plastic flowers in the simple, pottery vase; the lamp above our table had an amber shade. The Turkish popular music was too loud and we asked for it to be turned down. The waiter, nervously, brought our drinks.

"You're very quiet this evening," Erich said. "That trial?"

I nodded, but added that it was also my decision about staying in Holland that weighed on me. I was meeting Niek tomorrow, and it looked like directing the gallery was in the offing. As I went over the facts again it became even clearer to me how hopeless the plan seemed. Risk or security: my teaching position, my comfortable bourgeois condominium, my income and job security; on the other side the gallery, no certainty of income at all, and Sander and the risks of a modern-day boy-love relationship.

Erich said he thought Niek might even prove reasonable and that I should give him a chance tomorrow, but I could not imagine Niek giving up the reins just like that. His ego was too involved; he would try to keep some control and undermine whatever anyone was trying to do. Of course, I had to wait until tomorrow to see what really was in the offing. I could do it on my own terms, or not at all.

He offered this analysis: I was not Dutch and that was both an advantage and a disadvantage. I could remain a neutral party, not involved in the politics of the photography world. I did not know the subtleties of the language yet but I had international connections and collectors.

I offered my own additions: the gallery issue was really about money. I had some savings that I could fall back on, and the income from my apartment there was higher than the rent I was paying here, though if course it was not enough to live on. There was the advance for the book also, which I would receive as soon as I submitted the manuscript. But, I didn't really see myself as a gallery director, a business man: greedy, cheating people, ruthlessly competitive, American in the worst sense of the word, crass, self-serving.

Erich burst out laughing. "Well, if that's your image of a businessman!" I was embarrassed and he added, "Given what you've said, maybe at least the financial part isn't all that risky. In any case, risk isn't something intrinsically evil you know. The psychological theory at least is that at some point in our lives — how old are you, thirty-four? — one has to integrate risk into the psyche to continue to grow. It goes sometimes with a mid-life crisis, sometimes before, sometimes after. The theory at least is that a life that builds in healthy risk is a more creative life."

"You think I should take the risk then?"

"Oh, I don't know. It might be the right time, but then again it might not be. It might only be a kind of test run to get you ready for something in the future."

I thought that was a very odd thing to say, and did not respond.

He continued, "Besides, that's not the real issue, which we seem to be avoiding."

I did not want to get into it. I looked away from him, down at the table. But I did say, "Sander?", though it made me suddenly feel sad. I looked up and we stared at each other for a moment or two.

His face could sometimes be quite kindly. He said, with much concern, "Will... just let your instincts guide you. And after all, if you decide to stay it's the right thing, and if you decide to leave it's the right thing. Just trust your instincts."

6. The Paedophile Workgroup Meeting

The first person I saw as I walked into the meeting was Toon. He was sitting on a bar stool at the counter wrapped in animated conversation with a handsome teenage boy. An exhibition of someone's mediocre drawings of nude boys was mounted on the walls and as I walked around viewing them I said hello to the various people there I had met over the past year of attending. The lights were dimmed; Dutch cabaret music was playing in the background. The smoke had become nearly impenetrable and I pulled aside one of the drapes and opened a window, letting in a cold wet draft.

The workgroup meetings were held in a run-down building owned by the NVSH (Netherlands Society for Sexual Reform), the oldest of the Dutch sexological societies. It had reached its peak of more than a hundred thousand in the 1960s by giving out free contraceptives to its members but since then had dwindled to its current all-time low of under ten thousand. Nearly every city in the country still had an office, though some of them were very small, each office divided into various 'workgroups': naturism, family planning, transsexualism, paedophilia.

The sixteen Dutch groups totaled more than all the other

groups in the world combined, though it was hard to assess what that meant sociologically. Dutch tolerance was very complex, mostly it meant: 'I'll leave you alone if you stay away from my family.' Dutch tolerance was a matter of boundaries. Within your own confines you could be left alone, but only if you did not venture into a confine that was at odds with your own reality.

The open existence of paedophile groups did little to account for paedophilia as a phenomenon, which as far as I could see was at least as old as the Hittites. Society gave it different shapes at different times, fueled by the religious, economic and cultural debates of the moment, but the underlying sentiments were the same: the impulse to love and to bond, the impulse for personal freedom and growth, equally strong in the child as it is in the adult. To nurture and be nurtured, to create unions, to make poems, or photographs, and other creative objects: the language changed from era to era but the underlying desire and eros seemed to remain the same. It would not go away, nor could government really eliminate it. Suppression might force it underground. Governments are built on hubris, their arrogant belief that they have the right to control human nature to preserve the elusive common good. With all the discussion going on, perhaps paedophilia, much changed and chastened by the abuse debate, might somehow find a niche for itself in the world, though it might be nothing more than the uneasy, wary, tentative tolerance of the Dutch body politic.

It occurred to me as I stood at the window looking down on the tiny canal and the wet, cobble-stoned street, that the workgroup meeting was also something else. It was really a place where everything in the reality of the room contributed in some way to the sense of paedophilia. It was an unique space, a place where people of like reality formed a community for that reality. By extension the history of a subject, its literature and tradition, also became a space, as much a denotation of that reality.

I turned from the window and looked around. There was a table against one wall on which was displayed current literature on the subject, the various movement magazines from different countries and the most recent books, novels and studies. Two or three people hovered there, catching up on things and chatting with the person who tended the table. A video monitor was at the far end and a few chairs were grouped in a semicircle in front of it. A French video was playing that I had already seen twice, about a boy who goes to the country to live with friends of his mother while she has a baby. It was a lovely, tender film. Several men, besides Toon, sat at the bar, talking to one another. I saw a man passing around photographs of his summer vacation in Greece, mainly snapshots of boys in bathing suits. At one of the tables one of the men had brought his boyfriend, and another boy I had not seen before. They were playing cards, and the boy ran over to the bar to get drinks, peanuts and chips and things. He was Sander's age, as was his friend, and as he brushed past me he smiled, not at all self-conscious about being at a 'paedophile' meeting. I was still too American, too constrained by its sexual pathologies, ever to ask Sander to come with me.

Toon's companion at the bar left, and I went to join him. His lawyer thought that he would surely receive a three-month suspended sentence, but Toon was more pessimistic.

"In any case, I've been branded a criminal now." He looked quite dejected.

"Yes, but that's also a state of mind," I replied, but that was a mistake. It piqued the wrath underlying the surface.

"I'm now a criminal. A convicted rapist!"

"That's a bit severe."

"What do you mean? It's the law. That's what the law thinks of me; that's what this fucking society thinks of me. Why go around pretending anything else?"

"You don't have to believe that. You can somehow keep your innocence. The state calls your acts a crime, and you a criminal as a result. That's a social fact, but of course the other side of the picture is moral. The society, church and government call your acts a moral crime, but you don't have to agree with that. Somehow you can keep your moral innocence."

"What bullshit. It just doesn't work that way. If they want me to be a criminal, I'll be a criminal. This society is going down the drain. It's becoming like fucking America."

I must have felt threatened by his anger because I unwisely tried to make a feeble joke. "We can always start a new religion. The Congregation of Holy Boy-Lovers. In any case twenty-five per cent of the Catholic priesthood are paedophiles so we wouldn't have much difficulty recruiting."

I could see him grow even more angry, if that was possible. He started to say something to me, thought better of it, and walked away.

Erich came over to talk to me. He took me by the arm and drew me to the side, and said conspiratorially, "Now don't turn around suddenly and stare, but have you noticed that man over there against the wall?"

I maneuvered myself around until I could see who he meant. A tall, overweight man rather sloppily dressed in an old, checked flannel shirt and grey trousers was leaning against the wall by the bar. He had a black leather bag slung over his shoulder that looked more expensive than the sum total of all his clothing, including his watch. No one was talking to him.

"Well?" I asked Erich.

"He has a camera in his bag."

"Christ. A camera? Are you sure?"

"Yes. I saw him take a photograph."

"What should we do"

"Go over and talk to him, find out who he is, who he came with. I didn't want to do it alone."

"Do you think he's an undercover agent or something?"

"He's English. I heard him talking to Wim. I think he could be gutter press."

"What did he say?"

"Wim asked him how he had found his way to the meeting and he said that he had heard about the meeting by phoning the NVSH."

"Well, that's possible."

"Of course, that's possible. But it doesn't explain why he would take a camera to the meeting?"

We went over to meet him. He did not seem at all nervous. His right eye wandered a bit. I gave my first name, as did Erich, and he said his name was Andrew. He was from Manchester and the situation in England was 'bloody hell'. he had to get out of there and was thinking of moving to the Netherlands, but wasn't sure what kind of work he could do. He had worked at odd jobs and things, school bus driver, and had some computer skills as well. I said that people with computer skills seemed to do the best here, and that his European Community status would mean he did not need a visa to stay, just an income. Erich asked if he had ever been to a meeting before and he said he had not.

"The first meeting is sometimes a shock, I suppose," Erich said.

He shrugged, and I offered to buy him a drink. When I brought it back Erich was still drawing him out and as I handed the glass to him, Erich said, very loudly, "By the way, you have a camera in your bag and we don't allow cameras at meetings."

"I don't have a camera."

I said. "Well, you were seen taking a photograph. We don't allow that at meetings."

He was sipping his orange juice and looking at both of us. He was at least six inches taller than I, but others, sitting at the bar, had turned to listen, so we clearly had reinforcements handy. I don't think I had any doubts now about his being a gutter-press journalist.

Erich said, "Then you won't mind our looking in the bag."

"I most certainly would," he said, putting his glass down on a table at hand.

But then Toon came over and before any of us could make a move to stop him he tried to wrench the bag away from the man. The strap caught his shoulder and Toon had pulled it so savagely that the man spun sideways and lost his balance, stumbling against people sitting on bar stools. The strap broke; the bag flew open and the camera crashed to the floor. Toon picked it up and before the man had even regained his balance he had opened it and torn out the roll of film. He stomped on it with his foot crushing it. People rushed over ready to restrain either Toon or the Englishman, but both were oddly calm, facing off against one another.

Erich said to the man, "I'll show you out." We both accompanied him to the door. Someone retrieved his bag and camera and brought it to us in the hallway. He was trembling as we saw him onto the street. He pulled up his coat collar and tried to put the strap over his shoulder but the force of Toon's action had torn the strap and buckle away from the bag leaving a hole. He walked off without a word more into the rain.

I said to Erich, "What if he wasn't a journalist?"

"Then he's learned a hard lesson. You don't go for the first time to such a meeting and take photographs on the sly. What did he think? That no one would mind?"

"Come on, we need a beer."

We went back inside to the meeting. The cold, misty rain on my face had calmed me down a bit, but I still wanted a drink.

Someone had taken the roll of film and suspended it from one of the ceiling lights, a kind of hunting trophy. There was still a lot of adrenalin in the room. Erich immediately went over to talk to the two twelve-year-olds huddling at a back table. I thought, they see things like this at school, but still it is frightening. I went over to them and asked them if they wanted soft drinks, and they nodded. They were laughing nervously, confused by it all.

As I was leaving the meeting about a half hour later Matt came over to me and said, "I was going to talk to you about something this evening, but we didn't have a chance, with everything going on, so I was wondering if we could make an appointment and meet."

"What's it about?"

"I'd rather talk to you about it when we have time."

"In brief."

"Erich said you were thinking of staying here. I've been wanting to start an English-language paedophile magazine and was wondering if you would co-edit it with me."

I did not much like Erich speculating about my staying to Matt, and said, "It's news to me that it's so definite that I'm staying. I haven't made any decisions yet. I don't know if I'm staying or not."

"Well, I'd still like to talk to you about it. At least get your ideas. We need an English-language news-type magazine, with quality photos, mostly boys from twelve to sixteen, but something well designed, edited and printed. On a high level."

"Well we can talk about it, I suppose." I had my date book in my coat pocket and we made an appointment for the following week.

Part Five: Decisions

1. Saturday, March 3rd: The Gallery

I woke up this morning thinking to myself, "My God it's Sander's birthday party today and I still haven't made up my mind." I struggled out of bed and opened the living-room drapes. Gray again. The bells on the Rijksmuseum finished seven. What was I doing up so early? The party was not until four. At least I had bought his gift.

I still had to wrap it though, and finish my homemade birthday-card collage. I had found some new cuttings he would find amusing. I was quite proud of it: odd bits and pieces of comic books and cartoons, and a bit of a street poster announcing SANDER — THE GREATEST! — LIVE!, meaning Sander Vosberg, a well-known Dutch cabaret singer. I had carefully torn it away from the post.

Sander at ten had worn eccentric clothes sometimes. Floppy white fedora hats his uncle had found in some obscure part of Indonesia; underwear with red tulips or little red hearts; cutoffs that were too short and exposed a bit of him; or that secret time once when his mother was away and I stayed with him at his house and he pranced in a silken slip...

Sander at twelve? Difficult/cuddly, dependent/independent, beautiful/gangly, moody, funny, frisky, lazy. His new Walkman would be exactly what he wanted. And a witty tee-shirt I had thrown in for the bargain. The age of peer approval and conformity, of belonging. At the party today he would wear black trousers and perhaps my black, rap group tee-shirt, and the prerequisite running shoes by brand name only, Tarmac or Reebok or Adidas. Had he won the struggle with his mother so that she had broken down and bought him new ones? He would absentmindedly twist his digital watch around and around on his smooth wrist. No one else but I would notice the fine fleece of golden hair along his tanned arm.

But first there was a load of laundry and some shopping to do, the carpet to vacuum, the balcony door windows to wash, through which, in another week, the sun risen just high enough would finally begin to crest the building opposite. I turned on my computer and accessed my calendar: call Niek to confirm the appointment (would he really show up at the gallery?), call Erich Born to discuss my possible involvement in Matt's new magazine, and perhaps visit him next week, 'make a bloody decision!'

Sometime around ten I called Erich. The phone had hardly registered one ring when he picked it up. He was sitting at his desk preparing a trip to Jakarta. It seemed as if he had just returned from Morocco. He feigned an air of secrecy.

"Please don't tell anyone where I'm going. I'll tell you, but I don't want everyone knowing. I don't know why, but I seem to tell you everything."

We had just been together yesterday and he had not mentioned going away! I never quite understood the reasons for these boyish vows of secrecy. I had thought at first it was some sort of paranoia but he was also being playful and the meaning eluded me. He would be gone a month, perhaps even six weeks. I asked if we could have lunch on Wednesday to discuss Wim and Matt's plan, but he was leaving already on Thursday.

He said, "Their plan seems solid enough. They seem to have thought it through. Who knows, maybe they can make it work. I spoke to them last night after you had gone and they impressed me. They were very serious about it. On the other hand I don't think they realize how time-consuming it will be, and how little money they can get from it. What do they want you to do?"

"They more or less want me to be a co-editor, which probably means most of the editing work. What I was really getting at though was, what sort of a risk you thought I would be taking?"

"Maybe we shouldn't discuss this on the phone, but, yes,

I think there'll be some risk. I don't get the impression that they're the kind of people who want to test boundaries. It's merely going to be a news magazine, which we need, with photographs of young and older boys thrown in. I mean, if anything, I would have thought your objections to doing it would have been because your interests are more intellectual. How do you get along with them? Wim can be hard-headed and stubborn, but he's intelligent. Matt is neurotic and opinionated."

"They're better than some of the photographers around the gallery. But, how much do you think I have to worry about scrutiny, phones tapped, letters opened, that sort of thing; international paedophile network, conspiracies, investigations."

"There's always that threat, isn't there? You can take steps to minimize it: use another name, don't receive mail at your house, that sort of thing. I never thought that was the healthiest way, though, and if they want to know who is involved they'll find out. Personally, I don't see you committing yourself to that degree to a news-style magazine. Something more scholarly, more historical, yes. A history-of-record journal with an academic board. That's more you. Why don't you just do your own journal? Maybe we should talk about it too before I leave." He paused.

"I haven't even made a decision to stay, and I'm certainly not ready to discuss starting a journal."

"No, and I suppose these things should not be rushed. In any case it can certainly wait until I'm back from Jakarta."

"First things first," I said.

I had expected Erich to discourage me from doing the magazine with Matt and Wim, that is, to reinforce my own doubts. The last thing I had wanted was for him to throw another suggestion my way about something I might do if I stayed in Amsterdam. Especially something that needed major thought, not to mention risk. I felt as if Amsterdam were some sort of force field pulling me into its center. That was not what I wanted.

I immediately telephoned Niek. If we were going to meet

today to discuss the gallery we had better go ahead and do it. I had to take charge, get it all out of the way. He had not yet left the farm for the city and our meeting at the gallery was still on for one-thirty. He said he had spent the last two days getting together all the bills, receipts and invoices for the last couple of years so that I could have an accurate picture of where things stood financially. It might take a couple of hours to go over it all, and we could then go on together to the party at four.

By one, when I was ready to leave for the gallery, the cloud covering was breaking up into patches, letting through thick swatches of sun. I wrapped my red plaid woolen scarf twice around my neck and set out walking. I had reached footnote two hundred and three. Only seventeen more to check; the book could be finished by the beginning of the following week. Should I have a sort of Shaker birthing rite? Birth was the beginning of responsibility. This was more the feeling of relief, of clearing things away, of being able to start something new.

On a bridge near my house I stopped to watch the sun patches dazzle and darken the Rijksmuseum facade. Tourists babbling Italian milled around me. A man, woman and two boys caught my eye, apparently a family, standing at the corner of the busy street by the tram line. The older boy was about fourteen, thin, lithe, handsome; he had his arm around his younger brother's shoulders, a pretty child of eleven or so. He pulled him protectively out of the line of traffic and with his other hand reached across and touched his younger brother's cheek tenderly: a gesture which though small nonetheless defied at least one stereotype of unfeeling boyhood.

The gallery was only twenty minutes' walk from my house, in the basement of an elegant, eighteenth-century merchant's house along the canal: three steps down from the street, a Tolstoyan shop with photographers, not shoemakers, spinning myths. The building was owned by a friend of Niek's who provided the space at a very low rent as a favor to the foundation that officially owned the gallery. As with nearly everything in the country that had to do with photography it depended on some sort of direct or indirect subsidy. Monique turned from the computer and smiled. I smelled coffee. A glass of wine sat on the desk. Niek was surely here already.

The room was narrow, long, and very bright: beamed ceiling, highly polished wooden floors, walls white: peaceful, simple, orderly, unpretentious, still elegantly Dutch. Extra wide sliding doors in the back wall looked onto a well-tended, though, in this season, barren garden belonging to a group of houses that shared the expense of maintaining it: a variety of seventeenth, eighteenth, nineteenth-century rear facades opposite. It faced south, the sun still played its now and again game; the wind shook the glass doors, but it was warm inside.

The show there was one of mine: Bernard Faucon, 'Chambres d'Amour', color fresson prints of rooms and boys, intelligent narrative photographs, mysterious, symbolic. I had bought one for myself. A boy in white cotton boxer shorts is at the far right of the photograph walking out of a room filled with cobwebs and detritus. Is he leaving childhood, now decayed and lost? Is he enigmatically slightly erect? How should I read it? Does he step into another room now, of sexuality; has he already been aroused by some intrusive fantasy?

Monique was working on the mailing list. I had several faxes stuck in my letter tray: shop supply bills, an invitation to speak about early twentieth-century Dutch photographers at a photo fest-ival in Naarden in May, a response from a museum curator in Paris who said they would buy the group of Dutch photographs about Paris I had presented to him two months before — good news indeed. Where was Niek? I hadn't seen him yet. I wondered if he knew. I took out the calculator and figured out the profit: twelve thousand guilders. That was more than we had made in several months. I felt proud of myself.

Niek was in the back room, his own most recent photographs spread over the work table. The accounts ledgers were piled on a nearby chair. He had been doing a series of nudes of his mistress, Loo, who was now living full time with him at the farm. The new work was very large close-ups of parts of her body, especially the most intimate. It was obsessive, intense, shadowy, romantic, excessive. One especially caught my attention. It was a double-sized print; Loo's face was at the top left corner all in dark shadows hardly discernable, her leg was raised, the knee lit but the rest in shadows. It was a very good photograph but a bit old-fashioned, of the sixties spirit.

Niek looked worn, dark circles under his eyes; he had been gaining weight. The Dutch are such large people, I thought; he had so much mass. If he hovered over me I felt that the borderlines of his body, spreading far beyond him, might even block off the passage of air. His hair was thinning, his face was pale, his gold-rimmed granny glasses had small round lenses that only accentuated his expanse of face, all of it all too ready to twist into neurosis, his eyes too eager to go mad with too much intensity. Marijke had left him so that she could get on with her watercolors without having to bother about willfulness and needs and 'great art'.

He did not treat his photographs well, unless you made an aesthetic of torn and stressed prints. He wrote messages on them, scrawling across the front sometimes just his name, sometimes a line or a couplet of poetry. It was anachronistic, not something for the nineties. There were a hundred or so prints and he was obviously going through them for my benefit, pausing over some, putting some in one pile that he considered good, some in another that he claimed he would tear up, and even throwing some on the floor. Most were nudes of Loo, at least I supposed they were: parts of a body passed by, or parts of various bodies, in amongst them sometimes a landscape, or a garden, even one or two of Sander, one of which he extracted and laid aside.

"For you," he mumbled, and I was not sure he even meant it. The print was at least sixty by seventy centimetres in size and very dark and gray. Sander was lying on his side on some sort of oriental tapestry or rug or blanket, one could not tell exactly what it was, touching the base of his cock. Enough of his face was out of the shadows to show a stern, intense expression I recognized as his. It was a fine photograph and I hardly dared ask if it was really mine for fear he would play a game and withdraw it.

Niek shovelled everything into a pile and sank into a chair. He leaned forward and fumbling in his back pocket he extracted his wallet and drew from it a snap-shot. Throwing it onto the table, he slapped his hand down on it and said melodramatically, "There she is; a little beauty."

I'd noticed that he had a half-full bottle of white wine on the work counter behind us, and an empty glass near his elbow. I picked up the photograph: of a thirty-five or forty foot ketch. He poured himself another glass of wine with studied deliberation. He said, accentuating every other word dramatically, "That's it right there. That's why I'm giving you the gallery. That's my ticket to freedom."

He had bought the boat a few weeks before and it was now in the harbor of a village on the Ijslmeer not all that far from the farm. He was working on it day and night and once she was ready and outfitted he was sailing with Loo to the Dutch Caribbean for at least a year or two. An artist friend of Loo's was going to live in the house while they were gone.

"So, the gallery's yours," he slurred.

Fantasy or firm resolve? "I don't know if I want the gallery," I replied. "Anyway, when are you going?"

"No later than June, if we're crossing the Atlantic." He took a ledger off the top of the pile, opened it, threw it onto the table, and then poured himself another glass of wine.

"Look at that; you made more money in one sale this week than we made the whole year." So, he knew, I thought. "You're the one to do it. I don't want a thing from it. Just walk away. Maybe, later, when I'm back we can talk about it. Maybe not. An unconditional deal. That's what I'm saying. You take over the gallery, run it the way you want, if you can't make a go of it close it down. Do what the fuck you want. I'm out of here. In a couple of years we'll see."

"I have to think about it."

"Think about it!" he said disgustedly.

I did not want to make any decisions about an offer that was made drunkenly. "It's a tempting offer," I said. "Thanks.

When do you need a decision?"

But he did not answer. He went back to his pile of photographs and extracted another of Sander, which I found quite moving. He slid them both across the table to me, but did not say anything. Sander could have only been four or five when the earlier photograph was taken so Niek had obviously printed it recently for me. It was a head and shoulders bust, very brooding and a bit dark. Perhaps he had something of his father's dark side? He was biting into some kind of strap and pulling against it, his head pulled to the side in tension. He looked quite fierce, primitive, wild, intense.

"They're yours. Take them," he said.

I was suddenly upset and did not want to talk to Niek any more. I said I had some work to do and went out front to my desk: send replies to the faxes I had received, make a few phone calls, look through a German auction catalogue, fax the invoice to the French museum.

An hour or so later Niek wandered out from the back room. It was getting on towards four, and I was on the verge of asking him if he was going to the party but at the last moment thought better about meddling. He hovered for a moment over my desk and muttered something about not having a clear answer from me about the gallery.

"I need a week to think about it, so I'll have an answer for you by next Saturday."

He shrugged. When I left the gallery there was still not so much as a word about Sander's party.

As I was passing through the Dam Square on my way to Sander's an odd thing happened. It was as crowded with tourists as usual: crowds feeding the pigeons, listening to a spirited Ecuadoran music group that seemed to show up every spring and autumn here, grouping around a demented-looking person eating fire. The wind had died down and the sun felt quite warm and welcome. I stopped at the periphery of the crowd to watch. And, there were the Italian boys I had seen earlier. Village Amsterdam, I thought. I pressed through the crowd to get closer to them. They were certainly attractive. The younger boy especially had an air of grace and intelligence about him. They had changed their clothes. The older boy wore Levis, running shoes and a knee-length army green, hunting jacket; very macho. His black hair was a trifle long and flopped over his forehead inviting a hand to push it back and tuck it affectionately behind his ear. The younger boy was wearing pale yellow shorts that he had, perhaps recently, outgrown. They bunched up his long, brown, smooth legs and tightened around his firm buttocks. His nylon jacket was too thin; underneath I could only detect a tee-shirt. He was shivering. His older brother took charge, again all solicitude. He unsnapped his hunting jacket and drew his brother in against him, pulling the cloth around both of them. His brother snuggled into the nest, and at that moment, looking around like some protected fawn, caught me staring at them. He smiled sweetly, and I smiled back. Had he possibly remembered me from earlier in the day? I lingered for a moment more before continuing on my way.

2. The Party

At four, as I turned the corner onto Sander's street I could hear that the party was already getting well on its way: music blaring, child-ren shouting: whistles, horns, screams. A motorcycle roared past me on the street, a traffic helicopter hovered low overhead, a baby was crying in another house. The whole world was bedlam. I stopped on the street at the foot of the stoop, at least to wait for the outside sounds to subside. The weather was changing again, gray and impending rain.

Marijke opened the door, looking completely frazzled. Over her shoulder I glimpsed a child darting past, a profusion of large and small bodies. Sander had a number of cousins on his mother's side. Marijke was from a Catholic family, and her several brothers and sisters all seemed to have several children, none of whom I had ever met. Apparently she had invited everyone. It was louder than I thought. Children were chasing each other up and down the stairs, a balloon burst and a small boy started to cry, a glass of cola was spilt and an older girl ran into the kitchen to get paper towels. A woman was trying to organize a game but could hardly be heard and only chose to raise her voice further. I wondered if I really wanted to go in, and hesitated at the door.

"Who is everyone?" I asked astonished.

Marijke took my coat. "Half his school came," she said smiling wanly, "and the other half is family." She added rather defensively, "Twelve is an important birthday. I told him he could invite anybody he wanted."

"Where is he?"

"Upstairs somewhere. He and Michiel and some of his cousins are making a movie with the video camera for school."

A middle-aged woman Marijke introduced as a cousin, Marjan, came up to me with a tray of drinks and I took an orange juice.

"You're the photo person. From America. Marijke told me about you. You're Sander's friend." She glanced down at the box I was holding containing the Walkman and tapes. "You can put your gift over there with the others. We're going to wait until the cake is served to open them."

I suddenly felt selfconscious and out of place. What was I doing here? And what on earth had I been thinking? I had not calculated on a public opening of gifts. I had imagined Sander and me alone sitting on the edge of his bed quietly opening his gift together. He would throw his arms around me in a fit of gratitude and I would snuggle against his warm neck and smell scented soaps and oils, or some such romantic dream. No, it would not be acted out exactly like that. My head must have been in a cloud of scholarly footnotes.

Marijke must have sensed my befuddlement. She said, "I hired some entertainment, so it'll be better organized a little later. A clown and a musician. They'll be here around five." She glanced hopefully at her watch.

We passed through the living room on the way to the kitchen. There were two other women, and it seemed hundreds of children, but no other men. The doorbell rang again; my God, more children's voices. The kitchen door was open and we stepped into the garden.

"Were you at the gallery today?" Marijke asked, though I knew she was really asking about Niek. She drew a cigarette from a crumpled pack.

I nodded. "It was pretty quiet. I was there a couple of hours and no one came in."

"It's your show that's up now, isn't it? If no one is coming in, it must be disappointing to you, after all the work you put into it."

I shrugged. "About what I expected. There was a large sale to the Musée Carnavalet, so that sort of makes up for it."

She congratulated me. "Niek was going to make his proposal today, wasn't he?"

I proceeded cautiously. "Did he say anything to you about it?"

"About his boat? It sounds mad, but I think he should do it." She laughed in anticipation of her own remark: "It might make a new man of him."

I laughed. "Is it realistic, do you think? I mean, does he know anything about sailing?"

"Oh yes, he's a good sailor. Although I really think it's all some sort of competition with his brother who's done the same thing you know. I'm sure he can do it if he sets his mind to it; and stays sober. I'm all in favor of it. He really wants you to take over the gallery. He's like that you know about the gallery. He would first want to find the best alternative for it before leaving it. He can be scrupulously responsible. Dutch Calvinist. I'm not even sure he would go unless he thinks the gallery is in the best of hands."

"Well, it was a generous offer, but I have to think about it. I told him I would give him an answer in a week. It's simply a question of making a living. I have to sit down with paper and pencil and calculate it all."

I was beginning to feel annoyed again, as I had with Niek previously in the gallery. I was not sure whether Marijke genuinely wanted me to stay, or really wanted to get rid of Niek and wasn't sure if he would leave unless I took over the gallery for him.

I asked, "Where's Sander?" even though I had already

been told he was upstairs.

Marijke looked very irritated with me. She did not want the subject of the gallery dismissed, but knew me well enough to know that she could not force an answer either. She dropped her half-smoked cigarette to the ground and crushed it with her foot.

"I had better go back in," she said, "before they destroy the house. Why don't you check on them upstairs and see what they're doing? Where are those entertainers anyway?"

A neighbor woman was organizing charades in the living room. I took a sandwich from a tray and started upstairs. Perhaps I could just say hello and leave. He had already guessed what my gift was, and with all these people around I would hardly be missed. The voices were coming from the top of the house where Marijke had her studio, and I could barely believe she had given permission for them to make a movie in it. A steep ladder-stair ascended into the study; I poked my head cautiously above the floor level. Michiel hovered over a video camera set on a tripod. A small boy, sporting a thickly painted black moustache, dressed in a black cloak and dark brown floppy hat, was raising a wooden sword wrapped in tin foil above the head of a small girl. She was wearing some kind of massive black wig that looked quite like a pile of torn-up rags. Michiel ordered the action to begin and the boy brought the sword down to within an inch of the girl as she screamed. He looked up from the camera as I ascended into the room. Sander was not there but I thought he might be in the toilet or getting a prop so I stood around for a while talking to Michiel about the plot of their sword and sorcery video. They had finally decided on a plot, after several days of discussion. The boy was an evil magician who was trying to steal the fair maiden so that he could turn her into a black tulip and sell her for a million dollars. How this was going to be communicated via a video camera was not explained. After a few minutes when Sander did not return I finally asked where he was and was told that they thought he was in his room.

Michiel said he would come down with me because he

was thirsty. "Take a break," he said to his stars. He waited for me at the foot of the attic ladder.

"Sander is pretty moody today."

"Anything wrong?"

"I don't know. He won't tell me." He was wearing a black satin shirt decorated with red and yellow brocade, soft crushed black corduroy trousers, white running shoes untied. Without any hesitation, though not without considerable nervous shuffling and a bit of red face, he added, "Sander told me. About you, I mean." He looked down at his feet.

"Oh?" I said.

"It's okay. I mean, Sander... well." He was quite flushed and hesitating.

"It's all right, you know, if he told you. We spoke about it first and I trust you. So does Sander. You're his best friend. Along with me I guess."

"Yes... well... Sander said..." He could not quite look at me. He seemed to need more reassurance than I had already given him, so I added, "Well, Sander told me also, I mean about you and your... sort of things you have from your cousin..." I realized I was automatically imitating his own hesitant manner. "When I was about twelve my brother — he's older than me — he sneaked some stuff into the house and showed me..." If anything his face flushed even redder. But he looked up right into my face, biting his lower lip.

He whispered, "I asked Sander... I mean...," he exhaled. "Now, we talked about it... he said... well, it would be okay with him.. you know... he wouldn't mind... you and me." He had been looking down at his feet but suddenly, raising his head, stared straight at me and moved a little closer, close enough for me to feel the warmth of his body.

I wondered if he was taking it for granted that I would be attracted to him, which meant he clearly knew he was attractive. Of course he had gotten it right. I could not find anything to say immediately, but finally replied, "I think you're really attractive, and I really like you, Michiel. Especially, sometimes, when the three of us go to a movie and dinner together, and things like that." I felt a surge of tenderness, but did not act on it. "But I wouldn't want to hurt Sander's feelings." I did not want to hurt his feelings either. I lowered my voice and said, "I really like you. And I think you're really sexy."

He did not seem to need me to say anything more. He went downstairs without the matter being absolutely decided one way or the other.

I knocked on Sander's door, but there was no answer. I tried the handle but the door was locked. I knocked again. "Sander, it's Will," I said.

I heard him coming to the door. He looked quite sullen.

"Lock it," he said. "I don't want them coming in."

I locked the door. He lay down again and took up the science fiction book he had apparently been reading. I sat on the edge of the bed. He was frowning and pretending to read. I waited.

I thought I would try a variety of possibilities. "You in a bad mood?"

"No." He said it rather sharply.

"You're mad at your mother for something?" That was a good possibility because it happened often enough. He shrugged.

"Has Niek called you?" He shook his head. "That got you upset?"

"No. He's going away anyway. With Loo on a boat. And he's probably drunk or something. I don't care."

I wanted to take his hand but knew he was too sulky for that. I got up from the bed and paced the room a couple of times trying to concentrate. He had not asked me for his gift. He was not upstairs making the movie, or downstairs playing charades. There was no glass of cola on his night stand, nor dish of chocolates either. He was on his bed reading in the midst of his own party. Things were pretty bad. I folded my arms and looked down at him.

"I suppose I've done something wrong. You want to tell me?"

"No," he said. He folded back the page of the book and threw it on the bed. I noticed it was one I had given him. He swung his legs over the edge of the bed, sat up but did not stand up.

"How come you're not upstairs making the movie?"

"It's a stupid plot, anyway, and my cousins are little brats."

"I went up there to find you. I talked with Michiel a little."

"So?"

"He said you told him about us."

He was becoming more hostile. "So? I told you I would. What's the big deal?"

"There's no big deal. I'm just telling you he told me. So we all keep informed."

"I don't give a shit. He asked you, didn't he?"

They must have discussed it first. It began to make me angry. I said, "I told him that I didn't think it was a good idea having sex with him. I didn't want to hurt your feelings."

"I don't give a shit. You'd probably like it." I wanted to slap him. He looked up at me defiantly and said, "Anyway, you're going back to San Francisco, so it doesn't make any difference. What do you care anyway?"

"I do care."

"Right," he said sarcastically.

"I told you that I haven't made up my mind about going back yet, and I still haven't. But I have a job there, an income and I don't have one here."

"So when are you going? Tomorrow?"

"I told you I haven't made up my mind yet. What are you getting so worked up about anyway? If I don't go back you won't have a place to visit. I thought you wanted to come with me anyway."

He became angry. "That's stupid, isn't it. I can't go to San Francisco. You knew that all along."

He seemed suddenly older. Two days ago he had been acting a bit childish and ten again, but now a line creased his forehead and he had older concerns. I sat down on the bed beside him. I felt tired.

I said, "Well, for the umpteenth time, I haven't made up my mind yet, but when I do you'll be the first to know."

"Don't bother. I don't give a shit."

I was getting angry. "Yes you do. I know you do."

"That's what you think. But you don't understand anything. You don't know anything. You pretend to be so smart. So, why don't you just go? Like all of them."

I was stung. I couldn't speak. We were sitting on the bed next to each other but not touching or speaking. I felt it was all unbearable, felt selfish for concentrating on myself so much during the week.

"I do care," I said.

"You don't understand! You're..." he did not finish. He was biting his lip.

"I do Sander. I really do." And it suddenly became clear, the cloud of the week lifting. I looked at him, only a foot away, and added, quietly, almost to myself, "No. I can't. I can't go. I can't do that. I just can't go."

He looked at me suddenly, not sure what I meant. His face was flushed crimson red, sweat had appeared on his forehead and along his hair line, his eyes were swollen.

I reached over and put my arms around him. He put up no resistance and let me draw him against me. I said, "Oh, Sander, I love you. Don't you see that? I really love you."

He pressed his face into my shirt. He was shaking and he said, "I love you too. I really do. I don't want you to leave. Do you have to leave? Don't leave. You don't have to leave."

"I really love you," I said. "I can't leave you. We can work it out. You'll see. We'll work it out, but I won't leave you. Oh, God, Sander. I do love you."

3. Friday, June 15th. Letter to Dr Born

Dear Erich,

Your letter arrived today just as I was beginning to wonder if I should ever hear from you. I had not expected you to stay so long there. It took three weeks by air mail to reach me from Indonesia, but I see that it was not mailed from Jakarta but from somewhere called 'Oosthaven,

Propinsi Lamping'. The vivid stamps, teeming with tropical birds and turbaned people, the exotic names on the postmarks — a window flew open for me on the Dutch colonial divide. I had forgotten that the beginnings of Dutch oil wealth were in Indonesia. Perhaps, besides oil, color was added to Dutch life, as colorful as yards of batik. You said in your letter that you had contracted some sort of virulent stomach virus and were on an island recuperating. I certainly hope it is not too serious and that by the time this arrives you are completely better.

I was really happy to hear that your seminar had been a success. I knew it would be. I suppose it must have been something of a shock for the university students, many of them from the countryside, to suddenly find themselves in a course you say you dared to call 'Variations of Sexualities'. I'm eager to hear more. But, what did you mean when you said that Indonesian youth were 'puritanical'? That's a rather American term. Are they shy about hearing sex discussed in such a public and scientific way when normally it would have been couched in humor or banter? If I think of it, teaching such things as 'tribadism', 'third sex', 'scatology', 'paraphilias', 'sado-masochism', and horror of horrors, 'paedophilia', would probably be as much of a shock to my students in San Francisco (where we have such courses, as you know).

You will probably not be surprised to hear that it was a remark you made on the telephone ("You're right if you stay; you're right if you leave") that resolved my indecision about staying. I will be taking over the gallery as of the first of September, so I am spending a lot of time right now planning my first show, 'The Dutch Nude'. I had also remembered an archive that the photographer van Mekelenberg had: I asked if I could sell it, he said yes, and the Rijksdienst said they would buy it. The city is also extending its subsidy, though considerably less this time, so I shall be starting off on a good footing with some income and support.

The book is finished, though the publisher wants to

change the title. His suggestion is not completely terrible, *Tremors of Light: The Influence of Painting on Dutch Landscape Photography*. We are arguing about it and he seems to be winning. There remain the galleys to correct, two additional footnotes that have to be added, but all in all it is done.

I have in fact spoken to Matt and Wim about their magazine, the gist of which was that I said I had decided not to do it with them. I have enough to do this autumn with getting the gallery on a proper footing, but I think the real reason is that if I am going to take this kind of risk I would rather take it over a more scholarly journal, such as you and I discussed. Perhaps we can talk about how to go ahead with it upon your return?

I haven't seen much of Toon. Now that the court has ordered him to stay away from Ashok and his family he is very bitter and angry. I tried for a while to reason with him that his suspended sentence (as you predicted!) was quite incredible given the circumstances. But he doesn't want to hear comparisons between American and Dutch sentencing practices. He wants his hurt to be taken on its own terms — fair perhaps and not self-indulgent.

Thanks for asking about Sander. He and I are planning a camping trip to Denmark for a week at the end of July, as soon as his school year is finished. He is going through an odd phase. He has been making friends recently with younger boys, which he has not normally done, and I have been wondering what it all means. One of his new friends, a nine-year-old Surinamese boy, is with him quite frequently. They get along very harmoniously, sitting around on the floor playing rather younger games than Sander would normally play, with toys that have been locked away for a couple of years. Sander shows him a lot of affection, puts his arm around him, gets silly with him; they giggle and whisper together conspiratorially.

Is it Sander's attempt to hold on to his childhood, puberty encroaching, perhaps threatening? Or is this phase driven by a kind of nostalgia? I also sense an edge of sadness. It makes me wonder, do children subconsciously grieve as they approach or enter puberty? Perhaps they are energized and excited, but also mourn a little? He is sometimes irrationally angry, touchy about being called a child, moody and sad, then determined, as if gripped by the resolution to go forward. How little we know about children's emotional lives.

I have been telling him a story for the past several days that I am making up as I go along. He listens with total belief and with this peaceful, angelic look on his face. He wants every fact in the story to be exactly right. If I get the slightest thing wrong he is very irritated. Once, when his new friend fell down and skinned his knee, Sander washed the wound and put a bandage on it in a very gentle and motherly way.

Of course, he is going through changes: childlike and wondrous, stern and mature, surly and sharp. He has his own key to my apartment now, and sometimes when I return from the gallery I find him there alone, sometimes sitting by himself on the living-room floor playing with the Lego set I gave him a year ago, or cuddled up on the sofa with the cat. He has such a look of serenity on his face in these moments that I do not want to disturb him. Of course, minutes later he is badgering me and being an utter pest. His latest is that he refuses to eat his dinner at the table, and wants his meal in front of the blaring television. The other day he even went so far as to say that he would not use utensils to eat his food anymore, but would eat with his fingers; perhaps something his Surinam friend, who is Hindu, told him. Sander was always a bit difficult. He is saying now he wants to do something with his life that does not tie him down to an office; he wants to be a marine biologist. I am very encouraging.

He is in his 'healthy narcissism' phase. Anything that has to do with his body must be exactly right: a pimple that appears on his shoulder is treated as a crisis. When I take him shopping for new clothing all he wants are trendy tee-shirts. I want to buy him light blue turtleneck sweaters because I think they make him look sexy, but we end up buying some horrible black thing with a rap group message on it, which for him achieves the same image. The other day, when he was staying over, he suddenly decided he didn't want to take a shower with me anymore. He wanted a bath with almond-scented bath water, and much to my consternation he locked the bathroom door. I told him that I thought he was going a bit far, but he said he wanted his privacy. After the bath he walked around wearing only a white hand towel that barely tied around his narrow waist.

In other words, signs of hope and signs of trouble. A normal relationship? For days and even weeks on end things run along quite smoothly, and then something Marijke does, or a remark from Niek, will anger him and he becomes difficult to draw out. Last Saturday, for example, I telephoned Marijke to see exactly what time she wanted him home after dinner and she said, "Nine." This upset him a great deal. It seems that Michiel can stay out until ten or ten-thirty on Fridays and Saturdays as long as his mother knows where he is. I felt a bit caught in the middle. Certainly I was sympathetic to Sander. I had said to Marijke that I would walk him home as usual, so there was no danger of his wandering the streets late at night alone. But I was not entirely unsympathetic to Marijke either. Being home at nine is not such an unreasonable demand to make of a twelve-year-old, and I thought I should support his mother when I thought she was reasonable.

As we discussed it together I gradually came to understand that Sander's anger was not because of what he considered the early hour. Rather it was because his mother allowed no room for discussion. She laid the law down and did not want to discuss it. She did not feel that she had to. Her attitude was that when she said 'nine' she meant 'nine', and that was that. Sander wanted nine to mean the opening of the negotiation, the end result of which would, at least sometimes, be ten. Perhaps being caught in the middle is where I should be, no doubt an uncertain position but one that fosters dialogue.

Marijke's sister made a remark the other day which Marijke was quick to pass on to me, to the effect that, "Oh that American is still around Sander, I see," obviously disapproving. What could I say?

The past two weekends Sander has spent with Michiel and his schoolfriends, and although I am certainly encouraging him to be with his peers, I missed doing things with him. I found him once standing outside waiting for me, having forgotten his key. I had not been expecting him and had returned later than usual. He was very angry and said he had been waiting for an hour and a half for me to get back. I would have been back earlier if I had known that he was going to show up, but somehow he expected me to be there waiting, regardless. Perhaps as punishment, I don't know, a few days later when I tried to talk to him about his being angry with his mother he would not talk about it, and when I tried to insist he actually walked out on me.

Sander is not easy, but then there are times when a small gesture, a look, a remark lights things up. I was trying to explain some feelings to him the other day. He was sitting on a chair opposite me listening silently, and suddenly he walked over and pressed my lips together with his fingers. I stopped speaking; he leaned over and hugged me, and then went into the kitchen and made us both a cup of tea. It seemed like a very mature thing for him to do. Sander at twelve — reassuring. Perhaps he was right that time. It is a risk, but silence too has its place in love.

Warm wishes,
Will